I DO (NO'T)

ON ICE

I0618523

ALICE VL

I DO (NOT) – ON ICE

Alice VL

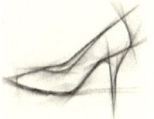

Copyright 2018

I DO (NOT)

Part 2

ON ICE

Alice VL

I DO (NOT) – ON ICE

Alice VL

HERE WE GO AGAIN!

Ally Bradshaw here ... again!

I am not going to lie, I have had two weeks of sheer and utter hell. It had been two weeks since I said goodbye to Daniel. Reluctantly. For two long, lonely and utterly wasted weeks, I had tried to establish some sort of routine for myself, with absolute no success.

I hadn't been out with Bianca, even though she had been coming around often. I had been avoided going out to the movies with her and basically just travelled between my apartment and work.

Still. I just couldn't stop thinking about Daniel. There wasn't a part of me that wanted to forget him and it confused me. Terribly. I didn't know what it was? I didn't know why each time I closed my eyes; my entire body began craving him. I could smell him. All. The. Damn. Time.

I woke up at night and caught a whiff of his oh so powerful scent. I missed him. Not me Ally, but rather my ever-growing, ever-increasing need for him. Urgh.

Michael had been pestering me non-stop. He called non-stop, he texted non-stop and he would drop by the museum or he would up at my apartment unannounced and at any hour,

I DO (NOT) – ON ICE

often at the most appropriate of times.

I would already be in bed at night, or still be asleep in the morning when he showed up as though he lived here.

He complained endlessly about Lily; her clinginess, her jealousy and more importantly, her insatiable appetite for him. Hang on. For him? For that under-developed, dwindling, crinkly, purplish, skew'ish and damn ugly part of him?

Lily needed a man. 'Oh, that's right; I can't really criticize her, can I? I took me twelve long and miserable years to discover how utterly disappointing he is.'

I had tried everything I could and, in my power, to give him the cold shoulder. I had tried ignoring his calls; pretend that I was not home and Gill went as far as to tell him I was not at work.

But, having said all that, I came up with a fool-proof plan to deal with Michael for once and for all. By the way, he never once showed up at my place with Lily. Whatever. I am over him. I am over that damn scary manhood.

In this instalment, find out how I dealt with Michael's sorry, whiny and scrawny ass. As you can probably imagine, it didn't end well for him, and he went as far as to involve my parents! That I didn't see coming and, in the end, didn't end well for me when my plan backfires miserably. Jerk.

On a more positive note, I scheduled an appointment with Doctor Walker, yes, Doctor William Walker – Plastic Surgeon. Remember him, the guy from the elevator who gave me

I DO (NOT) – ON ICE

his card? Yes him! Bianca and I ran into him at the movies one Sunday night after my two-week find-myself-period, and after a very brief, but oh so stimulating drink at his place, I went to see him under the pretense of discussing my girls with him, and a possible breast enlargement, or a lift.

Not really! Well, maybe the lift. I was seriously considering a bit of a tuck and a lift, but he didn't know that I had other intentions. Desires. Needs. I had a few one-night-stands set aside, that included him.

Only thing is, could he live up to my expectations. Could he measure up to Daniel? Why oh why did I walk out on Daniel? Why am I even mentioning Daniel here? This isn't about Daniel. This is about the Doctor William Walker. Him.

I hadn't seen Daniel at all during those two weeks. I hadn't run into him or knocked on his front door since the day we ended whatever it was that we had. I don't want to see him. Okay, I lie. Often, I'd hide in the coffee shop in the corner of the mall just to catch a glimpse of him.

There was something about my fireman in uniform that I just couldn't deny. Something so sexy, sensual, intimidating and overpowering. I would see Doctor Walker walk by too as he disappeared into the elevator. Aah, what a feast of masculinity.

Enough Ally!

My father called me a couple of days after my revenge rendezvous with Michael. Aah, I can't get that picture of Michael out of my mind. So, my father insisted I seek counselling for my questionable behavior. Everything aside, it was damn worth it.

Alice VL

I DO (NOT) – ON ICE

My parents demanded that I travel to Water Hills in Constantia for a good pep talk. For a little bit of Church and a whole lot of preaching. They were horrified by my behavior and when I learnt of Michael's enormous lie, I was crushed. Humiliated. Angry. I did not count on him lying to my parents.

I don't want to go, but I made a promise and swore to take the drive out to the farm for my three weeks of leave coming up in June. So here I am, still newly-single, almost two months after my divorce. I rely heavily on Bianca for advice, but my new-found freedom doesn't. The new Ally does her own thing and wants what she wants.

I did however, spend those first two weeks after my goodbye to Daniel shopping for newer, racier and so much more appealing lingerie, silk blouses, silk dresses and a whole lot more shoes.

I have thrown out my pj's. Yes! I have! I now wear nothing to bed. It was liberating. Sexy. Sleeping naked has introduced me to a whole new way of sleeping, and I sleep like a baby. Every night.

So, here we are! Let me take you through my highs and lows with William Walker as I continuously hanker after Daniel's intoxicating scent, chiseled chest, muscular arms and phenomenal lips.

Call me what you like, just don't call me drab, boring or ugly!

Ally!

Alice VL

PART 1

'What time is it? And who on earth is knocking at my door this time of the morning?'

I tried to coerce my sluggish eyes into opening, and knew for a fact that the relentless knocking on my door wasn't Bianca. It was still dark outside with not as much as a ray of sunshine peering through my bedroom window. 'Bianca always calls first.'

I glanced over at my mobile phone, still dazed and hardly awake yet. I squinted slightly, puzzled and perplexed when I realized that it was just a little after five.

'Seriously? On a Saturday morning?'

I didn't want to get up, so I laid back in silence, careful not to stir or make a sound. My eyes were barely open, and I was freezing. The sun wasn't due to rise for at least another forty minutes, and I hoped with all my heart that the knocking was nothing more than a dream. If it wasn't, it couldn't be important and I hoped that whoever it was, would give up and leave. I needed more sleep. I needed distance from the world, but more than anything, I needed solitude. I had just turned onto my side when I heard what sounded like an urgent and impatient banging on my front door.

'What the hell?'

Alice VL

I DO (NOT) – ON ICE

I was growing increasingly agitated by each knock that followed. It grew louder and louder as though whoever was on the other side of my door, knew without a shadow of a doubt that I was home.

'Shit.'

I honestly didn't need that kind of intrusion at that time of the morning, and I really didn't care who it was. I exasperatedly tossed my covers to the side and dragged myself out of bed wearing nothing at all, not even a smile.

I clutched impatiently at the robe that was draped over my bed. Having tossed it over me, I stepped impatiently into my slippers. It was one of the colder mornings by far. It had been raining all through the night and by the thunder and lightning that continued to roar around me, I knew that it probably wasn't going to let up soon.

'Why did I throw out all my pj's?' I criticized myself at once for failing to consider the subzero winters.

'Another knock! Seriously, what the hell?' I raced down the passage and switched the lights on as I grew increasingly alarmed with each step I took to reach my front door. Without peeking through the peep hole, I instantly opened my door out of sheer frustration and budding annoyance. I became highly irritated when I realized that it was Michael. Jerk.

"What the fuck Michael?"

Not appropriate, I know, but the only response I had to a man that I wished would disappear off the face of the earth. I was

Alice VL

I DO (NOT) – ON ICE

in no way at all to prepared to put up with Michael's uninvited show-up, just as he had begun showing up unannounced over the past two weeks. He would pitch up on a whim either at my apartment or the museum, and refused to leave until I was on the verge of throwing him out. 'Why oh why didn't I peek through the peep hole first?'

"Ally, seriously … you have to let go of that language. It's not befitting you."

"You're not befitting me, Michael. What do you want?"

"I had to come this way and past your place on my way to a showing. I just thought I could arm-wrestle you for a cup of coffee?"

"At five in the morning? Who shows houses at five in the morning? Who is even awake enough to commit to buying a house at five in the morning? These people have issues …"

"I do, and I have clients from out of town."

"You are such a liar, Michael. Seriously, what do you want?"

"Just coffee, Ally."

Flabbergasted and speechless, I shot invisible daggers at him and I swear, if they could manifest, he would be six feet under. He was still the scrawny, greying, self-absorbed asshole he was two months ago. His expression was of frustration and fatigue and I couldn't help but wonder if Michael had forgotten what it was like to be young and free, or had he become so absorbed in his own ambitions, that he was already dead?

Alice VL

I DO (NOT) – ON ICE

"Where's Lily?"

"Asleep."

"Yeah, that's what I thought."

"Can I please come in. It is so cold out here."

I didn't want to let him in, but while my head was still spinning, trying to find the appropriate words to send him packing in a calm and decent manner, an idea suddenly came to mind. An awful one, but oh, such a rewarding one, almost like a light-bulb, screwed in and switched on suddenly.

"Fine, Michael."

I grinned from ear to ear as I quickly planned out the details for what I had in store for him, in my mind.

'Brilliant. Ally 1 - Michael 0.'

I graciously stepped aside and made way for him to enter. Thoughts of how to perfect my seemingly already impeccable idea rushed around wildly in my head. Had I been anymore awake, I probably would never have even considered the fact that I had just been dealt with the ideal opportunity to take revenge on Michael. Like my grandma used to say, 'best served cold.'

'If this doesn't put an end to Michael's constant pitching up, I fear nothing will.'

If that didn't work, I knew that I would probably spend another long, excruciating and daunting twelve years trying to get rid of his pathetic ass.

He stepped inside and swiftly brushed past me. Michael appeared to be irritated, and walked steadily, stiffly and staunchly into the kitchen, almost as though he could still lay claim to me and my apartment. I instantly slammed the door shut and followed him into the kitchen.

Michael had already pulled out a bar stool from under the counter, and had placed his mobile phone and wallet on the kitchen top. I walked slowly as I tried to work out the finer details of a wicked plan running around in my head. It was so unlike me or anything I would ever have done a mere six months ago. 'I hope this works. It better work. Shit, I hope this works.'

After I switched on the kettle, I took out two coffee mugs and got the milk from the fridge. My robe opened slightly; nothing he hadn't seen before. 'Perfect.' I couldn't have planned that 'mishap' better if I tried; if I had rehearsed it a thousand times before, it could never have started out as perfectly as it had. It was a sign.

I pretended not to notice and didn't bother covering myself up while I nonchalantly waited for the kettle to boil. I turned around and grabbed a bar stool across from him.

"So, Michael ... what's all this about?"

"Ally, what are you wearing underneath your robe?"

He stared shamelessly at my almost revealing chest and could hardly take his eyes off me. I was not quite fully exposed, but he got the idea. At least, I hoped he did.

Alice VL

I DO (NOT) – ON ICE

"Nothing … why?"

"Oh Lord Ally. What has gotten into you?"

'No Michael, rather … who has gotten into me.'

I did my best to remain composed and relevantly poised while trying my utmost not to say it out loud, but I was dying to. I so badly wanted to blurt out that a fireman had swept me off of my feet while raising me up to heights I had never been to before, and in the process, exposed Michael for the selfish, self-absorbed, narcissistic and egotistical failure he was. I didn't.

"You've changed, Ally. I don't know who you are anymore?"

"Don't you? Did you ever? Don't sit there and tell me I've changed Michael when you're the one that screwed around on me with my best friend, in my home and in my bed."

"You are not the girl I married. You are not my wife."

I reminded myself to focus on my plan and instead of turning hostile towards Michael, I reached out for his hand and took it into mine. I couldn't shake the feeling of disgust that had suddenly crept up on me when I considered my intentions with him.

'This better work.'

"I'm not your wife, Michael … and maybe you just weren't paying attention to who I was?"

While I held his hand into mine, I was suddenly

I DO (NOT) – ON ICE

nauseated by his touch. My attention was drawn back to Daniel and the hands I had fallen in love with, but unable to fall in love with their master. Jolting myself back to reality, I cringed slightly, annoyed that Michael made no effort to free himself from my grip.

Secretly, I was relieved in the knowing that perhaps, just maybe, I could pull of my malicious scheme.

"I miss you, Ally. Lily watches my every move. She insists on the whole allure of romance such as dinners and roses. You know that I'm not that kind of guy? It's at times such as these that I realize you never really expected much from me. You were happy and content with the life we had made together."

'I was never happy, Michael.' I wanted to tell him that he made me miserable and made me see myself as a lesser version of myself. I wanted to let him know that for a short while, I had reached passions and heights I never dreamed I could be whisked away on; obsessions I would never have known had, had I still shared a life with him. I don't. Instead, I agreed with every word he said.

"Yep, I get it, and all you really want to do is screw? Right?"

"My God, Ally!"

I was loving every moment of Michael's repugnance. He was horrified, so I got up slowly and moved closer to him.

"Come on, Michael. We're both adults. Admit it, you just want to screw."

I DO (NOT) – ON ICE

His mouth opened slightly as he stared at me in disbelief. Michael's frown grew and his eyes began to squint. I had to remind myself over and over that I was on another life-changing mission and for my own sanity and peace, I had to see my plan through even though he revolted me. Even though he was the last man on earth I wanted around me, or in my apartment, or worse, in my bed.

I flashed him my most magnificent and seductive smile before I took his face into my hands. I bent down slightly and kissed him on his mouth. Appalled by the way his lips felt against mine, I traced his face and moved my mouth slowly over to his ears. I nibbled gently where I could at once, feel him wince underneath my mouth,

"Do you want to have sex with me, Michael?"

'You wish.' He remained quiet for what felt like a little too long. I didn't quite know what to expect from him and was slightly alarmed for just a moment.

"Yes."

His voice was throaty and shaky. I snickered softly and recoiled slightly to take him by his hand. I pulled him gently to his feet and dragged him seductively into my bedroom.

He didn't hesitate. He didn't protest. He didn't let out a single squeak and didn't say a single word. He didn't even smile. As though I was his new mistress, he followed me down the hall like a lovelorn mongrel on heat. My plan was working. So far.

When we reached my bedroom, I pulled him inside and

I DO (NOT) – ON ICE

turned around to face him. I was doing my utmost to seduce him convincingly when I chuckled softly. Not at him. Not at the prospect of engaging in an illicit sexual affair with my ex-husband, but because I knew exactly what I had in store for him and how it would play out. If it all went according to the plan in my head, it would be all worth it.

I bit my lower lip and slowly untied my robe. It fell to the ground, just as I thought it would. Sensually. Seductively. Michael stared at me while his eyes tracked my every move. He traced every inch of my body with his eyes, and when he stopped and stared at my thighs, a faint frown was evident on his face.

I knew what he was thinking. Never before had he seen such a perfectly waxed Ally Bradshaw.

I moved closer and slowly removed his jacket. I heaved it onto the floor and knew instinctively that he was secretly dying inside. He didn't say a word. Michael Bradshaw's suits never ended up on any floor. Ever. Anywhere.

Except here and for the very first time, at that very moment. He was the tautest, most uptight and rigid man I had ever met, and I was pretty convinced that he was the most conservative man I would ever meet. One crease on his jacket, shirt or trousers would be enough to send him spiraling out of control and into a hysterical panic.

I moved slightly to the side and deliberately stepped on his jacket. Michael noticed but again, he didn't say a word. I knew without any doubt that he was cringing inside and that his blood pressure was rising. I knew he was dying just a little as I carelessly trampled his perfectly pressed suit.

Alice VL

I DO (NOT) – ON ICE

'Asshole.'

With his tie in my hand, I slowly undid it. I recognized the tie as one I had bought him barely a year ago. It was enough to make me squirm at the old me. The tie was bland, boring and drab, just like I was.

'Yikes. Did I just call Michael bland, boring and drab?' I couldn't help but giggle softly.

"Ally …"

Michael's voice was raspy and sluggish. He stared at me and instantaneously, I detected the utter desperation and impatience on his face.

"Shhh …"

I pulled his tie out from under his collar and tossed it onto the bed behind me. My unmade bed. It was still dark outside, but the sun had just starting peeking through my bedroom window.

His shirt was perfectly ironed, and almost whiter than snow. I grabbed at it with both my hands and pulled with force. With all the strength I could muster up, I ripped aggressively at it. It had to work. It had to be enough to rip a few buttons off.

'Don't lose the moment, Ally.'

I prayed it would work. I had never done anything like that before; I had never tried to rip off any piece of clothing from a man, yet, the movies made it look so easy and oh so damn sexy.

'It worked! Holy shit! I can't believe it worked!' His

I DO (NOT) – ON ICE

buttons flew through the air in all directions and one-by-one. It was perfect. I was doing my best not to marvel at my success for too long, and pulled his shirt down over his arms, frantic to cage him and restrict his arm movements slightly. I wanted him standing there motionlessly, unable to move.

I noticed how Michael's horrified eyes tried to memorize the location of each button as they fell to the ground. I, in turn, secretly scrutinized his body. He was scrawny. Untanned and not a single carved or chiseled muscle. Not even one.

'Urgh.'

I kept a straight face and I kept going. I had to be convincing to shut him up and off for once and for all.

'Hold it together, Ally.'

I didn't make my abhorrence too obvious and allowed my mind to drift back to Daniel.

'Ally, stop!'

I did my best to banish that fireman from my mind, and out of my thoughts. His absence was torturing me and I was profoundly aware of an ache that would come and go. Nothing good could come from reaching out to Daniel again. I decided to rather take the pain sooner, than later. Maybe things could be different for us later. Maybe someday. Not that day.

I leaned forward and kissed Michael as timidly and gently as he would expect me to. Instinctively, I took in a deep breath trying to find Daniel's fragrance in Michael's skin. There was nothing. There was no scent to lose myself in. There was nothing to breathe in or get drunk on. He was just regular old Michael Bradshaw, hiding behind the aroma of fresh lavender soap.

There was no fire flaring up inside of me and no butterflies fluttering around in my stomach. There was nothing at all, and I was pretty sure there would never be any desire for Michael even if he spilled an entire bottle of cologne over himself. Never.

'Urgh.'

When my lips touched his, he kissed me back and for a second, I couldn't quite figure out what he was doing with his tongue. 'How did I never notice this before? What an idiot!'

I took his lower lip between my teeth and bit him. Gently. I could barely stand his tongue in my mouth and at that very moment, I wondered why it took me twelve years to notice all these irritations and short-comings about him?

'Because he was too busy reminding you about yours, Ally.' Michael retreated with downright terror written all over his face. He once again stared at me with skepticism and the bewilderment in his eyes was undeniable. I almost felt sorry for him. I almost, just almost felt bad for punishing him and having my moment of revenge on him. But, just as soon as the fragment guilt showed up, it passed. With all my might, I shoved him onto my bed and grabbed his tie.

As he fell to onto the bed, I climbed on top of him and when he placed his arms around me, I ran my fingers over his body. Michael squirmed as his arms tightened around me.

I DO (NOT) – ON ICE

"Don't touch me … if you touch me, I will punish you severely."

I whispered as I lifted his head and wrapped the tie around his eyes.

"Ally?"

"Don't even talk to me …"

I tied the nasty grey, white and navy tie around his eyes until Michael could no longer see me, or anything else for that matter. I couldn't help but stare at that tie in repulsion and realized that it was enough to put me completely off him.

'I need something to tie his hands with.'

"Lay still … don't move. I'll be back. In the meantime, relax and just imagine what's coming next … if you can. If your wildest dreams can go so far."

I whispered every so sultry in his ear before I got up and walked over to my dresser. I grabbed two silk scarfs and grinned.

'Oh Michael … I almost feel sorry for you.'

With both scarfs in my hands, I turned around and climbed back onto my bed. I took his hands one by one and began tying each hand to a bed post. I could barely imagine what was going through his mind, but Michael didn't say a word and complied without protest.

Once I was sure his hands were securely tied to my bed posts, I climbed back on top of him and slowly unzipped his trousers. From beneath his boxer shorts, I could feel that he was more than willing and definitely able to surrender to me. I slowly slipped down his shorts and stared for a moment. I was instantly revolted.

'How on earth was I happy with this for twelve years?'

Michael wriggled uncomfortably underneath me. He was growing impatient and grunted like a little boy, unable to wait his turn. I did what any revenge-seeking ex-wife would do and shamelessly, began teasing him. He whimpered loudly and lifted himself as his desperation grew.

"Not yet, Bradshaw."

While still running my hands over him, holding tightly onto him, my insides curdled like milk mixed in with lemon. I never wanted to be in that situation again. I could never go back to the person I once was; Michael's wife and lover. I was repulsed by Michael. The mere sight of him made me sick and suddenly, all the memories I had of my life with Michael were scarred, stained and grotesque.

Michael tilted his head back as he continuously and desperately tried to elevate himself. Up and down. Up and down, desperate to get me to submit to his arousal. 'Typical Michael, wham bam, thank you ma'am'. I was instantly annoyed but made an enormous effort to maintain the facade.

'Don't lose it now, Ally.'

He was nothing like Daniel. Michael evoked anger and disgust in me, as though I was caught up in a silent war with him.

I DO (NOT) – ON ICE

I wanted to beat him at his own game and destroy him in the process. Just as he had destroyed me not too long ago. For me, the rules between Michael and I had changed. I flinched at once when I thought back to all the I love you's I showered him with, and all the screw you's they had been replaced with.

Michael simply did nothing for me anymore and there was nothing he could ever do to discard the hatred I was feeling for him at that very second. I sat up straight and stared at him, appalled by my own behavior.

"Don't stop, Ally!"

Michael was seconds away from losing control of himself. 'I have to see this through.' I didn't want him to reach any summit at the expense of my body or under my watch.

"Tell me you want me, Michael …"

I whispered seductively as I pressed my body against his. I circled around his neck and nibbled slightly on his ear.

"Tell me you want to fuck me."

I hated using that word but I said it anyway. I cringed and sneered softly. That was not part of the plan. I knew into the very core of me it would almost kill Michael to repeat it back to me. He had barely used that term in all the years I had known him.

"Ally."

"Say it, Michael."

Michael squirmed again and lifted himself in frustration,

about to surrender wholly. By the dejected look on his face, I was almost sure he felt defeated.

"Fuck me, Ally. Fuck me!"

'Oh, that sounds awful!' He shouted out hoarsely and against his will as he lifted himself off the bed. My lips touched his before I pressed myself firmly onto him. I wanted to reassure Michael that I would soon be his.

"I'll be right back … don't go anywhere …"

"Come on, Ally … where are you going? I can't wait much longer …"

"I know you can't … but the best is yet to come …"

'That's right … what's to come will be most satisfying for me.'

I kissed him feverishly as I pressed myself forcibly onto him one more time.

"Come on, Ally!"

His entire body began to shudder and before I got up, I bit his bottom lip again.

"You better be ready when I get back."

I scolded him as he continued to quiver and writhe. I slid off him, and slowly tip-toed over to my dresser. Without making a sound, I opened my top drawer and grabbed a fresh set of underwear. I couldn't believe what I had done, but I was careful and utterly desperate not to alert Michael to my intentions.

I DO (NOT) – ON ICE

I tip-toed into my closet and quickly slipped into my underwear while grabbing a pair of jeans and a sweater. As though my life had been placed on a fast-forward setting, I was dressed in a jiffy. At the speed of lightning, I grabbed a pair of sneakers and without brushing my hair or teeth, I tip-toed back out.

When I reached the end of my bed, I savored the moment for just a second, suddenly tempted to take a snapshot as a reminder of how pathetic he is. I didn't. Michael looked pitiful while lying there with his blindfold on and his hands tied to my bed posts. For some reason beyond me, he was moving from side to side leaving me to chuckle into my sleeve.

I could only guess that Michael was working it, desperate to remain aroused and not lose his momentum for me, Ally Bradshaw; his ex-wife, the woman he had cheated on after twelve depressing years of marriage. As I stood staring at him, it suddenly dawned on me that Lily might not have been the first.

"Ally?"

Without any doubt, there was overwhelming evidence of panic in his voice when he called out to me and turned his head from side to side, desperate to hear me. The anxiety in his voice was apparent, but still, I didn't care.

"I won't be much longer you beast of a man. I just need another minute, Michael."

'Beast of a man? Holy shit Ally!'

I didn't know what else to say and had to think of

I DO (NOT) – ON ICE

something to keep him pacified and quickly.

"Hurry it up! Fuck."

'Now he can't switch off that word! I have created a foul-mouthed, disturbed monster.'

"That's no way to talk to a woman about to screw your brains out."

Michael squirmed again, but didn't utter a word.

Tip-toeing out of my bedroom, I grabbed my mobile phone and scurried down my passage. When I reached my living room, I slipped into my sneakers and grabbed my car keys. Without as much as a screech, I slowly opened my front door and prayed that Michael wouldn't hear me leave. Success! I slipped out and quickly closed my front door, leaving it slightly ajar.

I made a mad dash to the elevator just around the corner while dialing Lily from my mobile phone. Her phone rang only once before she answered and when I heard her sleepy voice, I smirked in pleasure.

"Lily speaking."

"Hi Lily. It's Ally."

"Ally?"

"Listen, Michael's car won't start. Can you come and pick him up from my apartment? I am headed to work and just can't drop him off at your place. Thanks!"

I ended the call rather abruptly, without giving her an

opportunity or an invitation to respond. I hoped she got to my apartment before Michael managed to untie himself. I hoped even more that she caught him in my bed; naked, tied, blindfolded and highly aroused.

The mere thought of finding Michael in such a compromising position instantly took me back to the day I had walked in on them. It was awful. I was distraught and it hurt like hell. For just a second, I re-considered my strategy. It was mean. Cruel. Heartless. It was a nasty thing to do to anybody and as I stood there waiting for the elevator to reach my floor, I questioned my ethics or lack of it.

Ally Bradshaw would never in a million years have resorted to such incredible malice even as far back as only two months ago. But, Michael did not back off. He just wouldn't let me get on with my life. He left me no choice.

'It's too late now. What's done is done.'

When the elevator reached the ground floor, I quickly dashed into the parking garage and to my car. I slipped into the driver's seat and stared straight ahead. With all the doubts that had suddenly entered my mind, I was still extremely sensitive to a sense of accomplishment that seemed to bury my hesitations.

'Asshole. Payback is a bitch.'

I burst out in uncontrollable laughter and pictured a horrified and shocked Lily finding him there. It would destroy her but at the same time, it would be all Michael's doing. I couldn't help but speculate on Michael's reaction to my leaving him there and calling Lily. The tears began streaming down my face as I laughed hysterically and visualized a panicky, scrawny and traumatized Michael coming face to face with Lily.

"Let him explain that to Lily!"

'Stuff him. Stuff her.

I wondered if they ever once felt any kind of remorse or regret while engaging in an extra-marital affair behind my back? I doubt it. While wiping the tears of utter gratification from my cheeks, I suddenly had no clue of what to do at that very moment or where to go when thankfully, Bianca came to mind.

'I just have to tell Bianca!'

I started my car and pulled out of the parking garage still wiping the tears of laughter from my face. As I pulled into the road in front of my apartment building, I could at once see Lily's car pull up. Hoping that she wouldn't see me, I looked the other way and drove right past her. I sympathized with her, but on the other hand, how I wished to be a fly on my bedroom wall.

I drove slowly. It was still early and I didn't really want to wake Bianca before the sun was fully out on a Saturday morning. When I pulled up into her driveway, I sat quietly for a moment and giggled softly.

When I couldn't stand it any longer, I climbed out with only my mobile phone and car keys in hand and swiftly walked up the path to the front door of her one-bedroomed cottage.

It was a beautiful place. Bianca's father bought her the house shortly after she graduated from college. From as early as she could remember, Bianca had adored the cottage hidden in the Hills of Willow County and she very quickly, left her mark and decorated it in her own kind of eclectic style. After her father passed away, she became obsessed with her home and swore never to sell the only thing she had left of him.

When I finally reached her front door, I hesitated. I hadn't noticed it, but I was nervous and completely frazzled. I stood silently and listened for anything to indicate that she was awake.

I listened for shuffles, footsteps and voices, but I couldn't hear a sound. Glancing down at my mobile phone, I realized it was just a little after six. I decided to knock anyway.

I knocked softly, not wanting her to be frightened or to wake up panicky and afraid. The last time there was such an early morning knock on her front door, was when she was informed of her father's sudden and unexpected passing.

I thought back to the day that she told me how it was that early morning knock on her door that frightened her almost to death. It was a kind of scare that entirely crippled and debilitated her. She continued to reflect on that day often, and some mornings, she would still wake up with a racing heart when any little noise around her woke her.

I waited for just a moment more before I knocked again, only, a little louder. Again, no response. There was not a sound or a shuffle coming from the other side of her door.

I dilly-dallied again, but lifted my hand to knock for a third time. Without warning, the door was yanked open by a not-quite-awake-yet Bianca who was wearing nothing but t-shirt.

I DO (NOT) – ON ICE

"Ally?"

Bianca was frantic to tie her hair and clear them from her eyes as she did her best to focus on me. I sniggered slightly when I noticed her frown,

"Sorry to wake you Bianca."

"What's going on? Did something happen?"

I was dying to tell her all about Michael, and what I had done. I wanted to blurt out that Lily had probably found him in an extremely compromised position, but first, she needed to let me into her house.

'Why didn't I pick up coffee on the way here?'

"I need coffee."

I smiled and immediately brushed past her before I strolled into her tiny living area. Bianca, still confused by my showing up so early and unexpectedly on a Saturday morning, closed the door behind me, and appeared almost as though she was frozen in time.

"Coffee, Bianca."

I giggled and made my way into her kitchen. As usual, her kettle was empty. I quickly filled it and took out two coffee mugs. When I turned around, Bianca was seated at her little dining room table, resting her head on her hands.

"You never come around here. Do you know it's not even six thirty yet? Don't you have coffee at your place?"

Alice VL

I DO (NOT) – ON ICE

"Ha ha! Funny girl! I would have coffee at my place, but … Michael's there … and so is Lily."

Bianca lifted her head and glared at me. The look on her face was priceless, and again, I so wished I could take a snapshot of that moment. It was a look of confusion, trepidation, astonishment but more than anything, the curiosity on her face was irreplaceable. I sneered and ignored the questions in her eyes.

"This time of the morning?"

"Oh, he's been there since five."

"What does he want with you this time?"

"Whatever it was, he certainly didn't get it."

"What did you do?"

I smiled again and quickly poured our coffee before I took an empty seat beside her.

"Don't you have bagels or something?"

"Check in the fridge."

"Aah, you are so predictable."

'Bagels first'. I shot up from my seat and opened Bianca's fridge, secretly wishing that my fridge was as organized as hers. Except for the bagels, there was fruit. Lots of fruit. Juice. Yoghurt. Cheese. Salad. Water. So much water.

But, I wanted bagels, my comfort food. I grabbed the

brown paper bag and plonked the bagels down on the dining room table in front of us. The marvelous whiff indicated that they were fresh. I grabbed two out of the bag and handed one to Bianca before a bit a chunk out of mine.

"Are you going to tell me what happened?"

Bianca was peering up at me as she again rested her head on her arms.

"He damn well woke me up at five this morning and it horribly annoyed me. Anyway, he came up with some excuse of showing a listing and that he was in the area. He supposedly just wanted a cup of coffee, and blah, blah, blah. At first, I didn't want to let him in ..."

"But?"

"As I stood staring at his stiff and staunch stature, all I could think of was that he cheated on me and for twelve years, he had me believe I was awful. He had me believe that I was lucky that he chose me and that I owed him for it. At one point after I discovered his relationship with Lily, I blamed myself and felt badly for Michael. I mean, I truly thought that I didn't deserve him. Anyways, then it hit me! I was none of that! I was a damn good wife and I would have done anything for him. He rejected me for no reason that was my fault and I should teach him a lesson. You know how he has been texting, calling and showing up unannounced lately?"

"Yeah?"

"So, I let him in. I pretended to make coffee and then ... I began seducing him."

"You did what?"

"But, not in the way you think, Bianca. Pretend seduce. I am not that much of a tramp."

Bianca at once sat up straight and stared at me. There was no way in the world I could miss the glowering on her face, or the grin that began to form all at the same time.

"And then?"

"I seduced him ... I led him into my bedroom. I had absolutely nothing on underneath my robe, so of course, I was completely nude when I let my robe fall to the ground. You know? Like in the movies ..."

"Uh oh."

"So anyway, I took off his jacket, his shirt and that disgusting tie I hate so much. And guess what I did next?"

"Oh, just tell me already!"

"I ripped off his perfectly ironed shirt. At least, all the buttons just about popped off! You should have been there! That look on his face when he watched each button fly through the air. He was horrified but didn't say a word!"

I couldn't help but laugh hysterically when I noticed the look of amazement on Bianca's face. More than that, I was pretty sure that there was an indication of pride in her eyes. For me.

"Shit, Ally. You're beginning to scare me."

I DO (NOT) – ON ICE

"So anyway ..."

I quickly bit off another chunk of the bagel and swallowed down a large sip of coffee,

"I literally tossed him onto my bed, and blindfolded him with his own, ugly tie. I tied his hands to my bedposts and you know ..."

"Oh no, Ally. Don't tell me you did it with him?"

I almost choked on my bagel. 'Who does she think I am? Sort of?'

"No, I have standards girl! But, I got him so buzzed that he couldn't wait to get it on with me."

"Ally! That's horrible! Why did you give in to him?"

"No, but hang on. I didn't. I wanted him to think that it was going to happen, and then I left him. Just like that, I walked out of my bedroom."

"You kicked him out?"

"No, I left. And on my way out, I called Lily and told her his car wouldn't start and asked her if she could pick him up from my place."

Bianca had just taken a sip of coffee when she spat it out and jumped to her feet. The look on her face was one I had never seen before, but not only incalculable, but highly entertaining. Whatever it meant, I was convinced that I would never live to see it on Bianca's face, ever again.

Alice VL

I DO (NOT) – ON ICE

"You left him, like that? Tied up? Blindfolded? And naked? Really, naked?"

"He still had his pants close by, but his manhood was wholly exposed. In retrospect, I wish I painted two eyes on with my lipstick."

"Ally Bradshaw! And then?"

"I left. When I pulled out of the parking garage, I saw Lily park in front of my apartment building. I left my front door slightly open, so she would have no problem getting inside. I just hope Michael wasn't able to untie himself. But, I did a pretty good job tying him up … I think."

"Oh shit. You know you're in deep shit now. Not as much as he is, but you are in deep, deep shit."

"Why? He cheated on me with her and then he wanted to cheat on her with me? He's an idiot. I actually feel a little sorry for Lily."

"I don't. She was your best friend and screwed your husband behind your back for who knows how long? I never liked that girl, you know that."

"Yeah … I know."

Bianca bit off another chunk of her bagel and stared incredulously at me. I smiled and gulped down what was left of my coffee before my mobile phone rang suddenly. When I peeked at the caller ID, I was just a tad bit unnerved to see Michael's name on the caller ID. 'Did I really think he was going to pretend it never happened?'

Alice VL

I DO (NOT) – ON ICE

"Oh shit. What do I do now?"

"Who is it?"

"Michael!"

"Just tell him to get lost. Or ... just don't answer."

I stared at my phone for just a few seconds longer before I answered his call,

"Michael ..."

"Do you have any idea what you've done!"

Wait. Hang on. What I have done? Michael was fuming and shouting at the top of his voice.

"Really, Michael? What I have done?"

"You are one crazy, psycho bitch, Ally."

"Yeah well ... you should have thought about all that before you came around to my apartment, uninvited and at five on a Saturday morning ... without Lily."

"You are not the woman I married. I don't like who you've become, and I will never forgive you for this. And just you wait until your parents hear what you've done!"

He was fuming. Livid. Enraged. Embarrassed. He sounded disappointed and I was sure I could detect a hint of sadness. Or, was it humiliation? I couldn't quite tell.

"I know you won't forgive me. I'm rather counting on

that. But Michael, just so you know, you are exactly the sorry excuse of the man I married."

He didn't say another word and when I heard the call disconnect, I chuckled softly. With my mobile still in my hand, I gazed up at Bianca who had erupted into a silent fit of laughter with tears streaming down her face. Not a sound came from her as she juddered hysterically.

I burst out laughing and tried with all my might to picture the impression that awaited Lily when she found him naked, tied up, blindfolded and almost certainly anxious. Again, I couldn't help but feel just a little pity for Lily.

Like me, Lily came from a strict, overpowering family with endless rules, high standards and unreasonable expectations. I often used to tell Michael how similar we were, and how similar our childhood was. I was sure that we were soul sisters, and I thought we'd be friends forever. I never in a millennium of years could ever have suspected Lily of having an affair with Michael. It never crossed my mind, not even once.

Lily was painfully shy. Proper. Decent. Ethical. Wait. Scrap ethical. I thought she was ethical. She spoke gently and slowly, and used perfect language. The pronunciation of her words was flawless. I couldn't recall once that I ever heard her cuss and I couldn't think of once when she had a negative attitude or something destructive to say about anybody. Perhaps that was why her betrayal hurt so much.

Lily was never interested in dating. Or, so I thought. She highly criticized cheating men, and women for that matter, and believed whole-heartedly in the sanctity of marriage. She would regularly tell me how terrified she was of the fact that a man might leave her broken-hearted someday.

However, putting aside all my feelings of disgust for Lily, I had to admit that she was beautiful. Lily was everything I was not, and so much more. Her appearance was crucial to her and she dressed to the tee with not a hair out of place. She scheduled her hair, nail and wax appointments a year in advance, and never missed one.

I had never known Lily to cancel a single appointment in tuning up her appearance. She would rather cancel a coffee or movie date with her friends, but never once compromised her appearance. She only wore dresses, but on the odd occasion that she would wear trousers, it would be a tailored pants-suit.

Lily would never be seen dead in a pair of jeans, sweater or sneakers. Just like Michael. The more I thought about it, the more I realized that she was Michael. A girl Michael. Snobbish. Uptight. Habitual. Boring. Miserable. Sad and unhappy human beings. Cheaters.

"So, Ally ... what now?"

"Now nothing. I can only hope he leaves me alone."

"Are you still seeing Daniel?"

Daniel. 'Sigh.' How I would love to see Daniel again.

"No. I haven't seen him in two weeks. I am slowly trying to wean myself off him. It's not easy, but necessary."

"I don't get you? The guy obviously likes you and wants

more, yet, you dump him the moment he starts investing in you and a possible future with you?"

"Bianca, come on! I told you I don't want that. I've just come out of what feels like a life-long, soul-crushing marriage. I like Daniel … a lot. I just don't want to be tied down again. I like the informality of it all. I like my freedom. I like that I don't have to answer to a man; to anyone for that matter. I don't want the pressures of a relationship and I don't want to create an expectation with Daniel. What we had was amazing. Liberating. Exhilarating. Erotic. Perfect. I actually don't know what to call what we had?"

"Oh, I do. Slutty encounters with a really nice guy who doesn't deserve to be treated like a toy!"

Bianca grinned from ear to ear before I burst out laughing again.

"I take offense to that! I never deliberately treated him like a toy and it's only so-called slutty if there is more than one man I am sleeping with!"

"I have no doubt there will be another, and another, and maybe another?"

I tittered sarcastically and slid my coffee mug over to her.

"Your turn to refill our coffee. And speaking of … I met a Doctor William Walker in Daniel's apartment building. In the elevator, actually. I am so sure he was flirting with me … especially after he handed me his business card."

"Ooh, really? Have you called him?

"No, not yet. I've been trying to come up with an excuse."

"He's a doctor, Ally. Pretend you're ill!"

I snickered evilly and shook my head when Bianca switched on the kettle.

"He's not that kind of a doctor. He's a plastic surgeon."

"And he lives in Daniel's apartment building?" Bianca's eyes were wide open.

"I know. That is rather odd? I would have thought he lives around here somewhere?"

"Why don't you go see him for a boob job?"

Her eyes fixed a gaze on my girls before I instinctively covered them with my hands, desperate to hide the fact that they were basically non-existent. 'I don't want to have them cut or sliced open.'

"I don't want bigger boobs!"

"Oh Ally. You need to get with the program and read between the lines; not a real appointment, a pretend one."

Bianca was brilliant. Scheming and conniving, but brilliant.

"Why didn't I think of that?"

She poured our second cup of coffee while grinning from ear to ear. When she made her way back to the dining room table, she slid my filled mug back over to me.

Alice VL

I DO (NOT) – ON ICE

"You need me, Ally Bradshaw! You are still so new at all of this! Oh, that's another thing. Are you taking your maiden name back?"

"Nah, I thought about that, but I actually like the ring Michael's last name has to my first name. Besides, I know it will just about end up killing him!"

"Aah … gotcha!"

"Do you think they have left my apartment yet?"

"Who? Michael and Lily?"

I nodded as I sipped my coffee. Bianca burst out laughing again.

"I am bloody sure they have!"

Bianca and I both polished down one more bagel with our second cup of coffee when I glanced down at my wristwatch. It was just before eight. I was pretty sure that Michael and Lily had evacuated my apartment and taken the walk of shame back to theirs.

I was not prepared for any of the drama that awaited me when I woke up that morning. I was never the malicious, vindictive type but then again, I wasn't the one to cheat on Michael with his best friend.

"I have to run. My apartment is unlocked, and I desperately need a shower and toothpaste. Shall we catch a movie tomorrow?"

Alice VL

I DO (NOT) – ON ICE

"Yes sure! Afternoon show?"

"That would be great!"

Bianca rested her head on her arms again when I placed our coffee mugs in her basin. I turned back to her and was suddenly enormously indebted to her, and her unconditional friendship and support.

"Go back to bed. I'm sorry I woke you …"

I hugged her tightly before I seized my mobile phone and keys, and rushed to get back to my apartment.

Alice VL

PART 2

When I reached my front door, I was slightly hesitant, but cautiously walked into my apartment. The door was closed but when I turned the handle, it opened at once. For a moment, I thought that Michael might have locked my door and taken my apartment keys with him. That, I would expect him to do.

I peeked around the corner and listened for the sound of voices, movement, footsteps or just any kind of shuffle coming from inside. There was not a sound. It was eerily quiet. I tip-toed inside and vigilantly gazed down the passage like an intruder in my own home. There was no doubt in my mind that I would surely die from heart failure had they still been there, waiting me in.

There was nothing. Complete silence. I turned back to my front door and closed it softly, making sure to latch it. Still on my toes, I walked quietly down the passage towards my bedroom. Still, nothing but silence. When I finally reached my bedroom door, I hesitated again. I peered in nervously and caught a glimpse of my unmade bed.

I tip-toed inside and almost trampled on broken glass. I bent down and realized that the broken glass was from a vase on my dresser.

'Lily. It must be.'

Alice VL

I DO (NOT) – ON ICE

I grinned from ear to ear and could only imagine what had taken place between Michael and Lily in my bedroom when she walked in to find him naked in another woman's bed. I would have given anything to hear how Michael explained himself?

I peeked over at my bed and noticed his tie still laying on my unkempt bed. I chuckled softly. I couldn't deny the utter pleasure of seeing the evidence of an apparent dispute in my bedroom. I peered into my bathroom and was finally convinced that they both were gone.

My bed sheets suddenly sickened me. I couldn't stand the sight of them or the haunting vision of Michael laying there, waiting for me to grant him sexual gratification. Hankering for me. Desiring me. Lusting after me. As though someone had stepped onto my grave, my body erupted into one gigantic shudder.

Once more, it was all about Michael. It was all about his needs and his pleasure, just as it had been throughout our entire marriage. I immediately ripped my sheets from my bed and was overcome by a significant cleansing that unexpectedly came over me; one I had never felt before.

It felt as though I was slashing and discarding Michael from my life for once and for all. I was glad Lily found him the way she did. I was happy that I did what I did. Michael was a cheater. Lily knew when she submitted to him the very first time, that he was a married man. Neither considered my feelings or the sacrifices I had made for Michael, why should I?

Instead of placing the sheets in the laundry basket, I wrapped them up in a refuge bag and place them in a corner of the laundry.

"Good riddance to everything Michael!"

I wanted a shower. I suddenly felt dirty and stained. After placing fresh linen on my bed, I climbed into the shower and stood motionlessly under the hot, running water. I was at once shut off from the rest of the world and thought of absolutely nothing.

In that very moment, there was nothing in the world I loved more than feeling the water flow onto me and down over my entire body. It was an indescribable feeling; almost as though I was being washed clean from my sins, from Michael, from my parents and from the woman I once was.

I closed my eyes and decided there and then that Ally Bradshaw would never again be the obedient, quiet, dutiful wife she once was. I would never be trampled on again. I would never, ever give me heart away so freely again. I liked my life exactly as it was in that very moment.

I had changed. The things I thought I once wanted, was nothing like what I wanted then. I wanted life. Freedom. Power. A voice. I wanted to be noticed. I wanted to be seen and heard.

I wanted to be admired. I wanted to be seen as sensual and beautiful. I wanted to be lusted after. Desired. I wanted my body to speak louder than my words. I wanted to have someone explore my body just as Daniel did. I wanted much more than Michael ever gave me. Again, my mind wondered off and drifted back to Daniel.

Alice VL

I DO (NOT) – ON ICE

'Why does Daniel always come to mind when I think of more?'

I savagely reprimanded myself for thinking of and lusting after Daniel even though he was just so damn hard to forget. I continuously relived our few short weeks together and I couldn't help but wonder if I would ever truly forget him. Not that I had to. Not that I must. Just for my own sanity.

I gazed down at my chest. They were a little small and hardly a handful in the smallest of manly hands, but they had never been a source of dissatisfaction before today; before Bianca suggested a so-called enlargement.

'Perhaps it's not a terrible idea. Even just one cup bigger?'

I quickly rinsed my hair and climbed out of the shower. Still wet and dripping, I marched over to the full-length mirror I had developed an unhealthy love and hate relationship with. I closely inspected the girls and cringed slightly. They were just beginning to sag a little and at the very least, could probably use a slight lift.

"That's it, Doctor Walker ... I am coming for you ..." I smiled and slipped into a strappy, summer dress.

'Ally Bradshaw ... you've got this.'

Alice VL

I DO (NOT) – ON ICE

I spent the remainder of Saturday deciding on how to approach Doctor Walker. I didn't want to make it quite so obvious that I was trying to sink my claws into him, but at the same time, I didn't really want a breast enlargement. Not that I thought I didn't need it, but to be honest, I have always been terrified of needles and hospitals. The best I could come up with, was a consultation for a lift that I probably would never go through with.

Michael and Lily were discreet and unobtrusive. I hadn't heard another word from them since that morning and I was relieved, but more than anything, I was convinced that I had dealt with him appropriately for once and for all. But, I knew Michael better than that. I suspected that he was overcome with degrading feelings of humiliation and rejection. Michael did not, in any way at all, deal well with refutation or shame.

His pride was hurt, and I, Ally Bradshaw, cold-heartedly bruised his ego. As long as Michael would live, he would never live that down. He would find a way to make me pay for setting him up for Lily to find, but I didn't really care. There was not much he could do, and there was nothing more I feared when it came to Michael Bradshaw. He was a prick. Period.

I slept in on Sunday morning and woke up just after nine. From the moment I opened my eyes, I knew that it was going to be a beautiful, sunny day. The clouds had all disappeared and the sun was out, shining brightly. It was the perfect day for a movie date with Bianca later that afternoon.

I was looking forward to meeting up with her later, but I cringed at the mere thought of possibly running into Daniel. I was powerless to resist him especially after two weeks with no contact. I missed him. I missed the way he would look at me, as though every ounce of breath was taken from him. Each time he kissed me, the world around me shut down, leaving just the two of us to wander around in the moment together. Daniel was a story I never wanted to end, and I hated that it did.

I had not been able to banish him from my mind and it left me feeling vulnerable and out of sorts, as though it was stretching out throughout my entire body. At times, I would be without purpose, and at other times, I would feel incomplete; like something was missing from me.

Desperate to reconnect with Daniel who was beginning to entirely engulf me again, I glanced down at my phone and scrolled down to his name.

'Just one message?'

I was frantic to convince myself that all I wanted, was to know how he was doing.

But, from somewhere deep within me, I knew that was not all I wanted. That could never be all I'd ever want from that fireman.

"No, Ally!"

I reprimanded my temptations and was highly irritated with myself when I angrily tossed my phone onto my bed. I slipped into a sky-blue summer dress and tied my hair into a loose braid. 'I need to schedule an appointment with Helen again.'

The reflection in the mirror berated me for allowing my

auburn hair to slowly begin to fade and become dull.

'Ooh, and it's definitely time for another wax job.'

I slipped into a slightly heeled pair of silver sandals, and when I glanced at my reflection in the mirror one more time, I unintentionally fantasized about Daniel tearing my dress off me before he covered my body with his gentle touch.

"Ally!"

I at once rebuked my thoughts and desires and tried to shake all thoughts of him and our past encounters. I had an eerie feeling that I would be doing so much more rebuking, berating and reprimanding in the weeks, possibly months to come.

Alice VL

I DO (NOT) – ON ICE

When I pulled up in front of the mall just after 4pm, I switched off my car and reached for my bag from the passenger seat. As I was about to open my door, I heard a bleeping sound coming from my mobile. I glanced down to see Bianca's text flashing on my screen.

"Oh, don't tell me she's cancelled?"

I quickly scrolled down to her message and was instantly relieved,

"Waiting for you …"

"Just pulled up!"

I tossed my phone into my bag and quickly made my way through the ever-familiar glass doors of Willow County Mall. I was careful not to make eye contact with anyone around me and I peered anxiously around, desperate to avoid Daniel. I prayed that he wasn't caught up in the same crowd I was.

"Ally! Over here!"

'Oh, thank goodness.'

I was delighted to spot Bianca almost at once and swiftly, marched over to her.

"Have you been here long?"

"No, just got here. So, what are we in the mood for?"

"I don't know? What's showing?"

"Let's see, Shutter Island, Harry Potter, Inception, Blue

I DO (NOT) – ON ICE

Valentine and Twilight Eclipse. Pick one."

"I am not at all into Harry Potter or Twilight. Any one of the others will be fine. You choose."

"I think I might like Blue Valentine?"

"Okay, Blue Valentine it is but only because of Ryan Gosling."

"Oh, Ally Bradshaw, you man-eater you!"

We both giggled as we stepped into the back of the never-ending line. My mind instantly drifted back to Daniel, six floors up. Instinctively, I lifted my head, eager to catch a whiff of his scent. I swear, I could smell that man a mile away. But, there was no trace of him. No scent. No fragrance. No nothing to indicate that Daniel was close and the realization of that void left me secretly disappointed.

I glanced around at the crowd standing in line, who just like us, were waiting to buy their movie tickets. I immediately felt a sense of familiarity when I spotted a man walking through the glass doors and realized at once that it was Doctor Walker. Without taking my eyes off him, I aggressively nudged Bianca.

"Look! It's him! Doctor Walker!"

I could hear the exasperation in my voice and was at once mortified by my behavior.

"Where?"

"There …"

I DO (NOT) – ON ICE

I shifted in beside Bianca and pointed in his direction.

"That blonde guy with the white coat on."

"Ooh, yummy! You should go over!"

I glared at Bianca, convinced that she was drooling.

"No ways! No, no, no!"

"Then I will!"

Bianca suddenly grabbed me by my arm and before I could successfully protest, she marched me right over to him.

"Yoo hoo! Doctor Walker!"

I was mortified when Bianca shouted out to him while lifting her arm to signal our presence. I wanted to die. Again, I wished the floor would open up below me, and swallow me whole. I wished for any evidence of Ally Bradshaw's existence to be swept into that hole and disappear forever.

He stopped dead in his tracks and turned around at once. Bianca picked up the pace and continued to drag a reluctant, embarrassed and suddenly highly introverted Ally Bradshaw behind her. Me.

"Hi."

"Hello?"

Bianca extended a welcoming hand before introducing herself, and once again, I was left stunned by her confidence.

Alice VL

I DO (NOT) – ON ICE

"I am Bianca and this is my newly-single friend, Ally Bradshaw whom I believe, you have met before? You do remember her, right?"

Doctor Walker smiled and took Bianca's extended hand before his eyes trailed over to me.

"Apparently, you met her here, in the elevator?"

"How can I forget?"

He reached for my hand and shook it gently. His hands were silky soft and warm, but firm. Strong. Exactly what I'd expect from a surgeon.

"Nice to see you again, Ally Bradshaw."

"Thank you. Nice to see you again too."

More than ever, I wished for that hole to open. Nice? What kind of a word is nice? I could almost hear my mother scolding me for using the word nice.

'Nice is something you can eat Ally. Seeing someone again isn't nice.'

'Oh mama. If only you knew how enormous my appetite is, and what all I eat. Nice. Should I have said, yummy to see him again?'

I grinned mischievously as I played out a possible conversation with my mother.

'No, Ally!'

I DO (NOT) – ON ICE

"Are you ladies here for a movie?"

"We sure are! Do you live here, Doctor Walker?"

"Uhm, Bianca …"

I whispered and nudged her all at the same time.

"Well, sort of. I'm not from Willow County. I am here for only three months until Doctor Richard Hanson gets back from a three-month hiatus. I live over in Sutherland and am only renting an apartment on the fourth floor temporarily."

Bianca poked me with her elbow and beamed.

"Oh?"

She was intrigued. Fascinated. Charmed. Captivated.

"I perform mainly reconstructive surgeries to children who are severely affected by disease. Little ones who are disfigured in war-torn countries and children who can't afford reconstructive surgeries. Basically, I work for nothing."

I melt. Seriously? Could this man get any better? I gazed into his arctic and almost frozen blue eyes and noticed a coldness in them, but just a moment later, I was met by a warmness that entirely contradicted what I saw only a second ago. It obscured any rationality I had, and bowled me over all at the same time.

I guessed him to be in his mid-thirties, but definitely older than I was. That was an instant plus for me. His face was covered in evidence of stories that included heartache and pain, long working hours and much discomfort. He was clean-shaven, almost clinical looking, but when my eyes fixed a gaze on his mouth, I couldn't help but wonder how his lips would feel against mine.

My eyes tracked down to the white T-shirt hiding beneath his coat. I was instantly introduced to a carved chest just waiting to be freed from that T-shirt. With nothing else but chiseled chests and succulent lips on my mind, I continued to trace his body down to what I imagined to be a perfectly ripped abdomen.

I made a concerted effort not to linger too long, and when my eyes continued to trail down, I visualized an equally mightiness hiding from the world.

'Oh boy.'

My thoughts were impure and dangerous, and when I gazed back into his eyes, I was at once unnerved by his unanticipated glare.

'Did he just bear witness to me scrutinizing every inch of him?' I was horrified. Surely, he couldn't know what I was thinking, or could he?

Bianca was flirting shamelessly on my behalf, and all I could do was imagine Doctor Walker underneath me, on top of me and against me.

"You ladies are welcome to join me for a drink later, after your movie? It gives me time to have a quick a shower and tidy up a little."

He smiled at Bianca, and then he grinned in my direction.

I was suddenly in awe of his striking smile accompanied by perfect, pearly whites.

"We would love to!"

I grabbed and squeezed Bianca's arm, desperate to shut her up,

"I am sure Doctor Walker's had a long day behind him. It's Sunday."

"No, not really. I have only one surgery tomorrow, and the rest of the day I see Doctor Hanson's patients."

"Would you consider a private patient?"

'Oh Lord.' This was so typical of Bianca. I knew her so well and I knew without any doubt, that she was eager to get me an appointment with him.

"Perhaps?"

"Oh, it's not for me. I don't need anything. It's for Ally. She just told me yesterday that she wanted a boob job. I mean ... a breast enlargement."

"Really? Well, you have my card Ally Bradshaw. Make an appointment and we can schedule a consultation. So, I'm in apartment 411. It's a corner apartment on the fourth floor. Will I see you ladies later?"

He smiled at Bianca before he turned back to me,

"I sure hope you will come?"

I DO (NOT) – ON ICE

I could at once feel the blood rushing to my face and I knew exactly what I looked like when the heat rushed throughout my body. I instantly turned the color of a ripened, almost rotten tomato.

"Thank you for the invitation."

I smiled cordially, and tugged Bianca at her arm.

"Oh, we'll be there."

I yanked at her and when Doctor Walker finally nodded, turned around and walked away, I pulled her towards me. I was horrified.

"Bianca!"

"What? He is hot, Ally!"

"He is, isn't he? But, we didn't have to make it that obvious!"

"Yes, we did. He is so into you. How could you not see how he was staring at you? And when I said about the boob job, he couldn't keep his eyes off your boobs!"

"Rubbish, Bianca!"

I immediately folded my arms and instinctively covered up my girls.

"What if I run into Daniel?"

"So, what? Say hello, how are you … and move on!"

I DO (NOT) – ON ICE

"Yeah, I can't avoid him forever, I suppose ..."

Blue Valentine was a total disappointment and lost me within the first ten minutes. Other than catching short glimpses of Ryan Gosling, there was nothing much that kept my attention. Not wanting to spoil it for Bianca, I sat quietly and glanced over at her often,

'This is the last time she chooses a movie. I would much rather be six floors up with Daniel.'

'Wait. Hang on. I meant, four floors up with Doctor Walker,' I corrected myself straight away. Perhaps, the movie wasn't so terrible. Perhaps, I was so distracted by Doctor Walker that I was deliberately finding fault with the film.

When the movie finally ended, I tugged at Bianca, and suddenly remembered the last time I pulled her out of the movie theatre. I couldn't wait to run up and see Daniel.

"Sheez Ally! Hang on for a second!"

"You know I'm claustrophobic and that crowds suffocate me. I just want to get out before everyone starts pushing and shoving us."

"Liar, you want to go up to Doctor Walker!"

"Whatever!"

When we exited the movie theatre, Bianca casually slotted her arm into mine before we strolled nonchalantly through the mall to the elevator. Bianca excitedly pushed the button and I secretly prayed that Daniel didn't appear when the doors opened.

I squeezed her arm tightly against me and was instantly anxious when the doors opened. My heart was racing. My hands were trembling. I was vulnerable, and I didn't like that I had no control over the situation.

'Oh, thank goodness.'

The elevator was empty, but I couldn't help but feel like it was a close call and that it was nothing more than luck. I reminded myself that luck too would run out sooner rather than later and that I would have to be so much more aware and cautious of my surroundings.

Bianca and I stepped into the elevator before she animatedly pressed the fourth-floor button. I was edgy, jumpy and panicky.

When the doors finally opened on the fourth floor, Bianca pushed me out when I hesitated, and followed me out into the hallway. I glared at her when she began to snigger softly. She brushed past me before we hurriedly made our way down the passage, and into the corner to apartment number 411.

"I'm not so sure this is a good idea, Bianca?"

All I could think of was Daniel who was a mere two floors up. I was unsettled and wholly intimidated.

"We're two. We'll be fine!"

Bianca rang the doorbell and within seconds, Doctor Walker appeared in front of us, dressed in jeans and a black T-shirt. He looked dashing and smelled clean, fresh and almost clinical. He appeared to be relaxed, rested and oh so sizzling. I smiled bashfully while Bianca continued to dissect him with her eyes.

"Come in. Did you enjoy the movie?"

"Sure did."

Bianca grinned and walked past him and into his apartment. He turned to me before I hesitated for a moment,

"The wine's chilling …"

I frowned nervously and walked in slowly. I was not quite convinced I wanted to be there, and when he closed the door behind me, I glanced nervously around his apartment. It was scarcely furnished, and clean. It was exactly what I would expect from a doctor; a plastic surgeon who would be leaving soon.

"This way …"

He swiftly walked past me before I followed him into the kitchen where Bianca had pulled out a kitchen stool and made herself comfortable; as though she had been there a hundred times before.

I couldn't help but notice how similar the layout of the apartment was to Daniel's. I detected an almost exact replica of his place and again, I thought of him and again, I missed him.

"I have a bottle of red chilling. Can I pour you both a glass?"

I DO (NOT) – ON ICE

"That would be great!"

Bianca leaned forward and comfortably rested her elbows on the kitchen counter. She was totally unfazed by the fact that we were in a stranger's apartment, about to engage in social chatter which would be encouraged by wine. I slid onto a stool beside her and placed my bag on the floor below me. 'De Ja Vu.' I was restless and not quite as comfortable in Doctor Walker's apartment as I was the first time I was in Daniel's. I sat up straight and waited patiently for him to pour our wine.

Doctor Walker reached into an overhead cabinet and took down three glasses which he filled to the brim.

He handed Bianca a glass, and then he handed me one before he picked up his and lifted it to us,

"Cheers. It's nice to finally meet people in this town."

"What? You haven't met anybody yet? How long have you been here?"

Bianca was stunned. By the look on her face, I could at once detect the disbelief in her eyes.

"Nope. This is my third week here but honestly, I haven't even had a day off to take a tour."

"Oh, that's such a shame, but typical of Willow County. By the way, you're not missing out on much."

"So, Bianca, what do you do for a living?"

Bianca placed her glass on the kitchen counter and

leaned forward,

"At the moment, I design websites. Before that, I worked with Ally at the museum. That's how and where we met."

"You work at the museum?"

Doctor Walker was interested. I smiled timidly.

"Actually, she manages it."

"Very impressive. I assume that history is your thing?"

"That's true. I am fascinated by history."

"So, Doctor Walker, you really don't get to see any boobs or vaginas?"

'Oh Lord. Did she really just ask him that.' William Walker burst out laughing and placed his glass onto the counter next to Bianca's. I on the other hand, was about to choke on mine and clung fiercely to my wine.

"In the early years, I saw many. And yes, the answer to your next question is yes."

Bianca frowned and glared at him,

"What would that be?"

"Are they really all unalike and unique?"

"Oh, Doctor Walker, you must have been asked this question a hundred times before?"

"Please call me William. I sure have been. I didn't study

plastic surgery to alter a woman's body. All I've ever wanted to do was give each child a chance at a normal, functional life, even though they can't afford it."

'Is this man for real?'

I sipped on my wine before Bianca's mobile phone rang suddenly,

"Hello?"

I noticed a puckered brow as her mouth slanted downwards, instantly apprehensive.

"No that's alright ... I'll be right there."

Bianca ended the call and turned to face me,

"I have to go. My house alarm has gone off. It's probably just the neighbor's cat, but the security company is waiting for me outside my house to do a walk-through with me."

"I'll come with you!"

I immediately shot to my feet and placed my glass on the counter before I reached for my handbag,

"No, don't be silly. I'll call you, okay?"

"Bianca, I can really come with you?"

"This happens all the time, you have no idea how frustrating it is. No point in spoiling both our evenings. I'll call you later."

I DO (NOT) – ON ICE

When she winked at me, I knew that Bianca had faked that phone call and that she probably had someone deliberately call her.

"Have fun! Thank you for the drink, Doctor Walker."

"You're welcome. I'll see you out."

Bianca kissed me on the cheek before she followed the striking doctor out to the front door. From where I was sitting, I could hear them talk through Bianca's giggles. I just couldn't quite make out what they are saying.

When William Walker walked back in, he quickly made his way back around the kitchen counter.

"I hope she'll be alright?"

"Oh, Bianca will be fine. I'm more afraid of the one that crosses her."

I chuckled softly and gulped down what was left of my wine.

"So, Ally. What else is there to know about you?"

He refilled my glass, and I dithered,

"Not much. I work for the museum. I am recently divorced. I have no pets, or anything like that."

"Recently divorced huh? How long were you married for?"

"Twelve years."

Alice VL

I DO (NOT) – ON ICE

He almost choked on his glass of wine, and quickly placed it back down on the counter.

"Oh wow! What happened, or shouldn't I ask?"

"You can ask. He cheated on me with my best friend."

I gulped down on my second glass of wine he had since poured me, and gazed back at him. William Walker was staring at me with a pitiful look on his face. 'Oh no! He feels sorry for me!' I was horrified.

"Don't look at me like that. It turned out to be the best thing that's ever happened to me."

I erupted into an uncontrollable fit of laughter when I noticed him glower. He smiled sadly and continued to frown questioningly.

"Still, what a bummer."

"No honestly … it's not the cheating or anything like that, that bothers me. It's the life we had. The man he was. The woman I was. I am glad it's over."

I paused to take in a deep breath,

"What about you Doctor Walker?"

"Please Ally, call me William. I'm not your doctor."

"Not yet."

'Oh Lord. Did I say that out loud?'

Alice VL

I DO (NOT) – ON ICE

He smiled again and placed his elbow onto the counter before he rested his chin on his hands,

"Never married. I was engaged once, but with my working away and all around the world, things just sort of fizzled out. She is a city attorney, so we ended up seeing less and less of each other as the years went by."

"Years huh?"

"We were engaged for eight years."

"Wow! That is a long time."

"But, my kids are my priority now."

"Oh? You have children?"

"My patients … they're like my kids. You don't have any?"

"No. Thank goodness for that! I can't imagine sharing children or visitation with Michael. It would have complicated things way too much."

That came out with way too much respite and way more enthusiastic than I had meant it to be. Not really. That was exactly how I meant it. I just didn't want him to know that. Yet.

"I mean … with Michael and I divorced and not on the best of terms, I am glad we didn't bring children into this."

"Yeah. I get that."

'Oh, thank goodness. I felt like an evil bitch a moment ago.'

Alice VL

I DO (NOT) – ON ICE

"So, the other day when I ran into you in the elevator?"

"Oh that. I was just visiting a friend on the sixth floor."

"Oh right. So, you don't live here?"

"No, I live out at Willow Hills. I have an apartment over there."

"So, Bianca said something about a boob job?"

That escalated way too quickly. I wanted to die again. 'Really? Now?' I could once again feel the heat rush to my face and again, I imagined my face the color of a bright red tomato.

"It was just a thought. I may not enlarge them, perhaps just opt for a tuck and a lift."

William got up from his seat and slowly walked over to me. So much of what was happening at that very moment, felt eerily familiar and similar to my first meeting with Daniel. I bowed my head when my heart began to race irrepressibly.

He turned my stool around to face him and examined my girls with his eyes.

"I'll be the judge of what you need. May I?"

I nodded shyly. 'Of course, you may, Doctor Walker.'

He placed a hand over my breast and made slow, circular motions. He lifted it slightly and squeezed gently.

"It's so misleading with this dress of yours. Do you mind?"

Before I could respond, he slid his hand in under my dress and wriggled his way in under my bra. I could do nothing more than shake my head and watch him closely; I didn't mind at all. Again, he was a complete gentleman; a typical doctor when he examined me even though I could feel sudden and unexpected tremors run down my spine. 'Good grief, Ally. Could you play a little harder to get?'

My lips were becoming dry and coarse while his hand was warm, silky soft, strong and ever so gentle. All I could think of was a sculptor's elegant hands caressing my delicate chest.

Without taking his hand off me, he lifted my chin with his other, just enough to meet his eyes,

"They are impeccable."

He leaned forward until his lips touched mine. Softly and gently, he teased my mouth with his. I opened my lips, ready to take his tongue into mine, but he hesitated slightly. I pressed my lips against his and placed my arms around his neck. He pulled me onto my feet and wrapped his arms around my waist.

He kissed me more enthusiastically, and when I closed my eyes, I smelled him into the very core of me. I couldn't quite decide whether he smelled of rain or whether his whiff reminded me of the ocean. There was nothing artificial about the way Doctor Walker smelled; clean, fresh albeit, a little clinical.

William's hands traced my spine, over to my hips before he clasped me firmly and pressed himself forcefully against him. I could feel his body hunger for mine as he tightened his grip around me. I want that. I want Doctor William Walker underneath me.

He recoiled suddenly and stared at me in bewilderment, as a slight hint of awkwardness brushed over his face.

"Wow. I am so sorry …"

He was mortified and ran his hands bashfully through his hair. I was surprised. Disappointed.

"I'm not …"

I took his face into my hands and kissed him again. After hesitating initially, he kissed me back and I welcomed his tongue into my mouth.

William seized me up suddenly and carried me into the living room. When he placed me down, I slipped out of my sandals and could feel the soft, shaggy rug below my feet.

I stepped back slightly and pulled the straps of my dress down. I turned around and moved my braid to the side of my head. William slowly unzipped my dress before I turned to face him again. The dress fell to the floor, and landed around my feet. I undid my bra, and let it fall onto my dress before I walked closer to him; my hands quivering slightly. 'I am getting so good at this.'

I lifted his T-shirt before he took over from me and pulled it off over his head. He leaned in and kissed me again before he lowered me to the ground. I didn't hesitate even for a moment, and laid down on the shaggy carpet. He bent down and found a spot beside me, hovering slightly over me. With his elbow resting on the floor, he rested his head in one hand while his other hand gently traced over every inch of my body.

Alice VL

I DO (NOT) – ON ICE

"You feel like silk. You are beautiful, Ally ... you shouldn't want to change a thing about you."

'Beautiful. He said I was beautiful.' I kept still and remained quiet as he slowly moved over me with his hand. When he reached my thighs, I squirmed slightly. Each warm touch over my body ensured a gentle jolt down my spine. He kissed me again and slid on over me. He pressed down onto me with his jeans still on.

I anxiously searched for his zipper, and when I found it, again, he took over and unzipped his jeans. I want him exposed. I tugged at his jeans until he pulled them all the way down, releasing one leg at a time. I placed my hands over him and was pleasantly surprised that he was wearing no underwear.

'Oh my, Doctor Walker ...'

He pushed himself against me and again, I was met with strong tremors rushing throughout my body. I lifted slightly before he took over yet again and freed me from any garments that were left on my body.

He stared at me while his hands began discovering parts of me that were undiscovered and dormant until I met Daniel. 'Daniel. Shit.' I quickly banished Daniel from my mind when William began taunting me. Provoking me. My body began to crave him; I needed him. I could barely stand the torture a moment longer.

"Doctor Walker, I am ready for that shot."

"Are you?"

Alice VL

I DO (NOT) – ON ICE

"Yes."

"Alright. Just close your eyes, this won't hurt a bit."

He gently pressed down on me before I whimpered loudly.

'Oh boy.'

This plastic surgeon was undoubtedly enormously endowed. Immensely. Vastly. Every inch of me welcomed every inch of him.

I grabbed onto him as he pushed ardently and brisker against me. As he became fiercer and stauncher, I began to judder slightly. I felt a familiar, excruciating pulsation make way for a sensation I had been introduced to only weeks before. I was relieved. I was thankful. I was profoundly delighted that those magnificent sensations were by no means at all, limited to or restricted to Daniel alone.

It all felt comparable, yet slightly diverse and tingling sensations wholly overpowered me; parallel to a gazillion tiny bubbles under my skin that popped up bit by bit each time he shifted.

I was not quite prepared for the distinctive, unfamiliar sensation that began to build up inside of me. I didn't think it could get any better than what I had undertaken with by Daniel. I had no clue that there was a high, more advanced and elevated than I had been on before.

Almost like a new drug; it appeared to be improved, enhanced, and perfectly blended for an extraordinary, addictive and astronomical high.

One more shift. One more powerful shift was all that was needed to introduce a whole new level of exhilaration. My legs began to shake violently and fold instinctively around him as a million explosions inside me turned my body into one immense, fierce spasm. He continued to hold onto me as my legs tightened around him and my hands pressed into his back. I tilted my head backwards and desperately tried to stifle the sounds coming from my mouth. Sounds that became echoes and that I was only beginning to recognize them as my own.

Again, without catching a single breath, surprising ambiances began to intensify again. It was like a never-ending but piercing rise, that took me higher and higher. There was no likelihood of relaxing or catching my breath. There was no interruption, no ending and no coming down from the summit he had taken me to. A new peak was in sight and a brand-new pinnacle was about to be reached.

As my body began to adjust to its new altitude, my entire body constricted. Everything was different. Every sensation was so much more intense than ever before. William slid his hands in underneath me and raised me slightly to keep me firmly against him.

I buried my head in his shoulder and when the flare-ups began again, I sniveled loudly into his chest. He held me firmly against him as his grip tightened around me while his own breathing became gaudier and rapider.

He paused suddenly when his entire body began to twitch. With all his might, he strengthened his hold on me and grunted softly under his breath. I eased up slightly and squeezed my legs firmly around him one more time as I came down from a trance I had never been in before.

'This just gets better and better. What just happened?'

In that very moment, I wondered if there were any limits to erotic gratification and subsequent elevations. What were the boundaries? Why would anyone place restrictions on sex? I suddenly couldn't quite fathom why anyone wouldn't explore the enjoyment, fulfillment and deeply stimulating act of the freedom intimacy had to offer.

Why would someone want one partner for the rest of their lives? Intimacy with Daniel was deeply sensual and fulfilling, but with William, it was extraordinarily enchanting. I couldn't wait to do it all over again with the irrefutable champion of highs, Doctor William Walker.

He lifted slightly, gently kissed me as he tugged me firmly against him and hugged me tightly.

'Oh no, I don't want to cuddle.'

I hoped with all my heart that he wasn't a cuddler. Or emotional. Or sensitive.

William rolled over and stared up at the ceiling with a massive grin on his face. I spun around onto my side and gazed at him. I wondered what he was thinking, but I didn't want to ask him. I didn't really want to know.

"We should do this again." I blurted out all of a sudden.

I DO (NOT) – ON ICE

'Oh Lord, Ally.'

He immediately rolled over until his face almost touched mine. He placed an arm over me, and grinned self-consciously,

"You can say that again."

I smiled and tapped his nose gently before I sat up and reached for my clothes.

"Your bathroom?"

"Down the hall, first door on the left."

Thankfully, it was dark with only the kitchen light reflecting into the living room. This man was after all, a plastic surgeon; the body expert and they greatest judge and critic under the sun. I didn't really care what he said; I was pretty sure that somewhere in his career, he had created the perfect breasts and reconstructed a vagina or two. Ally Bradshaw was not one of those, but she sure wasn't boring.

With my dress in my hand, I scurried down the corridor, fully aware of my exposed behind. When I reached the first door on the left, I walked in and locked the door behind me. I placed my dress on the vanity and quickly glanced around me.

Almost sterile. It all smelled almost too clean. I grabbed a bar of soap that quickly foamed under hot water. I dabbed the foamy soap all over my body, and with a face cloth hanging over the shower, I sponged myself down.

I stared at my reflection in the mirror and noticed my untidy braid. I pulled out the band that still desperately tried to keep my mane together, and let the curls fall down my back. I beamed. Contradictory to my first meeting with Daniel, I didn't scold myself. How could I when I had just been to paradise and back, twice?

My dress slid with ease over my shoulders and I was secretly pleased that I chose that dress for my movie date with Bianca. I smeared a blob of toothpaste on my finger and rubbed vigorously against my teeth.

'There we go. Almost new. I should carry a toothbrush and a hair brush with me. I should carry underwear too. I am so new to this.' I was so clueless.

I hadn't quite discovered all the tricks yet, but I was getting there, learning fast. I quickly made a mental note of items that should always be in my bag before I chuckled at my reflection and promptly walked back out into the living room. William had climbed back into his trousers, but remained shirtless as he stood there, pouring us each another glass of wine.

"Oh damn. I so much preferred you stark-naked." He whispered ever so seductively when he glanced at me.

'What a charmer!' His hair was disheveled, and his smile was broad and exquisite. I didn't think it was possible before, but when I looked into his icy eyes, there was a hint of green in them that reminded me of spring and freshly cut grass.

Doctor William Walker was hot. Fine-looking and oh, so delightful. I gazed over at his shirtless chest and driveled all over again.

Alice VL

Sculpted, but not quite as carved as Daniel. Robust. Flawless. There was nothing more than a handful of blonde hairs on his chest, and just like with Daniel, I was tempted to run my fingers through them.

'Really, Ally? Daniel again?'

William made his way into the living room and sat down at the edge of a couch, holding a glass of wine out to me.

"Thanks."

I gulped down the entire glass and placed it on his coffee table.

"So, I had a pleasant evening to say the least, but I really have to run."

"Really?"

He immediately got up and made his way over to me.

'Why do I keep running away?'

"I work tomorrow and have so much to do before then. Thank you for a wonderful ... uhm ... evening."

"Oh no, Ally Bradshaw ... thank you."

He placed his hand around my neck and pulled me closer to him. He gently kissed me, and when I caught a glimpse of his hands, I was again, in awe of their beauty.

They were soft, smooth and beautiful. Exactly the kind of hands I wanted on me. 'In surgery. That is.'

Alice VL

I was slightly disappointed by the fact that I couldn't quite assess the totality of his physique. There was still a fraction of mystery to his manhood but I was counting on a next time to discover the unseen that was hiding in those jeans.

'Why oh why Ally? Why must you see each man you ever come across in his entirety.'

Who would ever have thought that that would be my thing? Ally Bradshaw's weakness. After the depressing sight of Michael's scrawny, tired, purplish, limp and frail him dangling towards the floor, every other man just seemed more beautiful, like an expensive art piece to me. A magnificent, incalculable sculpture in human form.

Besides, I could no longer ignore how these two men completely outweighed and surpassed anything I had ever known before. Incalculable pleasure. Boundless indulgence. No heartache. No strings. There was nothing more, but pure decadence at its finest. Point.

"You have my card. Call me."

He placed an arm around my waist and led me to his front door. 'Wait. Hang on. He doesn't want my number?' He wasn't asking me to stay. He wasn't at all offended by my leaving and didn't express his feelings of being objectified. I like this doctor, a lot.

When we reached the front door, he opened it and turned back to me.

"I am so glad Bianca had to leave."

Alice VL

I DO (NOT) – ON ICE

William leaned in and planted a kiss on my forehead before he stepped aside and made way for me to walk out.

"Me too."

After I had slipped into my sandals, I casually strolled out through his front door.

I turned back one last time, and waved harmoniously,

"Bye."

William lifted his hand and waved before he shut the door behind me.

Alice VL

PART 3

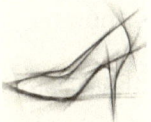

I huddled as quickly as I could to the elevator and was at once relieved when the doors opened without delay. I was not quite a fan of the so-called walk of shame and was convinced each time, that the world could see right through me and know intuitively what I had been up to, as though it was carved into my forehead.

I stepped in and was suddenly entirely unnerved and intimidated to find Daniel standing there, looking even better than I could remember. I could not even begin to imagine the cruelty of the universe as shame and disgusted slowly crept in and overwhelmed me. He was fully outfitted in his uniform, and I guessed at once that he was about to go on shift.

"Daniel ... hi."

"Ally? What a surprise."

'You're telling me?'

"I was just here ... visiting ... a friend."

"Right."

"Are you on your way to work?"

"Yep."

I DO (NOT) – ON ICE

Silence. Self-consciousness and unnatural discomfort followed.

'He knows. I bet he knows.'

My indiscretion with William must have been written all over my face. I had no idea of what to say next, and I could barely look him in the eye.

'He knows.'

"How have you been? Any new lovers?"

Daniels voice was croaky. Throaty. I couldn't quite decipher his tone. I much preferred the silence and I would much rather have taken the elevator on my own. I didn't want to answer him, but I could hardly ignore him either.

"Not seeing … technically."

"Oh, did I say seeing? I meant … screwing."

I instantly bowed my head in shame. 'He knows.'

Daniel was wrathful and noticeably hurt. He more than likely still believed that I used him. If only he knew how often I thought of him; how I compared him to every other man I met and how I evaluated Doctor Walker by the standards he had set.

Daniel had no idea that his compelling scent drove me wild and that sometimes, that was all that I hungered after. It overpowered me at times, and more often than not, I craved him so badly.

"Well, as long as you are happy with your chosen life, I

can see no reason why you shouldn't do what you want, with whom you want."

I nodded hesitantly and when the elevator doors opened, I was immensely relieved. I immediately turned my back on Daniel and walked out as quickly as I could. I knew that he was behind me, and short of running, I tried to blend in with a crowd in front of the movie theatre.

I was keenly aware of Daniel's sorrow. I felt guilty and a little sad. I felt responsible for the fact that Daniel still felt as though I used him. I was once again painfully sensitive to Daniel and his intoxicating fragrance and I realized again that I turned to clay around him. The younger, attractive, intimidating, captivating and appealing Daniel Sotherby, the fireman whose hands had stolen my heart.

I didn't want to turn around and evaluate the distance between us. I prayed that I was closer to my car than he was to me. A slight lump in my throat formed, and I couldn't quite understand my emotions.

'You just feel guilty, Ally.'

I struggled to convince myself of the fact that what I felt for Daniel was nothing more than loyalty, gratitude and friendly affection. Nothing more. When I reached the glass doors of the mall, I gazed up into the sky. It was raining. It came pouring down and lightning began igniting the sky. I clutched my bag tightly against me and ran over to my parked car. The rain had mercifully diluted the tears that had begun to roll recklessly down my cheeks. 'What the hell, Ally?' Raindrops hit my skin softly, with care, as though it knew of the adversity that had created a vicious storm inside of me.

I barely reached my car when I heard Daniel call out to me. I jolted and pretended not to hear.

"Ally. Wait!"

I fumbled with my keys and just as I was about to open my car door, I was instantly aware of Daniel gripping forcefully at my arm. I turned around and stared at him. I was excruciatingly aware of the tears that were still shimmering in my eyes, while secretly indebted to the rain crashing down on us.

'Why is Daniel upsetting me so much?'

I couldn't take my eyes off him. Through the blinding rain and the deafening sounds of thunder and lightning, I could smell him, and he drew me back in. I wanted nothing more than to feel Daniel's arms around me. I needed his skin against mine, and I missed his touch.

His dark eyes were exposing the storm that was creating havoc in his eyes. They flashed with annoyance, anger and wretchedness. It hurt.

'What are your eyes trying to tell me?'

My heart skipped a beat and my hands began to shake violently. Never has Daniel Sotherby looked so good standing in front of me, towering over me and standing underneath what seemed like a torrent coming down on him.

"I'm sorry, Ally."

I DO (NOT) – ON ICE

"You don't have to apologize."

My voice was breaking up and all I wanted to do was hide in a corner and cry. I wanted to crawl into his chest and disappear in his arms. I couldn't fathom why I was suddenly so heartbroken as an unexpected, unavoidable tear escaped and rolled down my cheek. I prayed he didn't see it.

"I do. This isn't who I am. I don't want to make you feel bad, Ally. I am just hurt and I think my ego is a little bruised. I know you didn't come here to see a so-called friend. I can smell him on you Ally, and it stings."

I bowed my head in shame and as a result, I became angry at Daniel.

"What do you want form me, Daniel?"

I became enraged while my heart began to hammer ruthlessly. I was hurt too. I was outraged. My stomach hurt, almost as though the butterflies Daniel had once sent me were dying one by one inside of me. I was angry at myself. I didn't understand my feelings and I never wanted to feel like that again. That was never the plan and I could never have predicted any of the emotions that my heart was introducing me to. I didn't understand anything. I didn't want to see Daniel again. Ever.

But, I did want to see him again. I did want to look into his dark eyes, again. I was not ready to abolish Daniel from my mind. I was turning into my own worst enemy.

"You, Ally! Just you! I want to take you back to my place and keep you there, with me. I am not ready to let you go. I hate that it was so easy for you to walk away from me, and I hate that barely two weeks later, you have moved onto someone else. Who does that? Why can't you give us a chance?"

"I am not built like that anymore, Daniel! Not anymore. I don't want that! I can't be cage in again. I just can't."

"I will never hurt you, Ally. I swear it. I will never do to you what Michael did to you. Just give me a chance. I know you feel something. I can see it in your eyes."

"You are seeing wrong … but you're not wrong! You are the guy that opened up a whole new world for me to explore. You Daniel, walked me through a gateway into a world I never even knew was out there. I do care, you're right, and that's why I left. That's why I don't want to see you again and that's why Daniel, we can never be friends. I don't feel the way you do! I don't want what you want! I like things as they are and if I end up in the arms of a thousand other men, then that is on me!"

Daniel leaned forward and placed his arms around me. I rested my head against his chest before he held me tighter. I was moments away from surrendering to him. I was mere seconds away from handing myself back to Daniel.

"Then … I won't stand in your way, Ally. I hope you find whatever it is you're looking for. Michael sure did a number on you."

"I'm not looking for anything. I have what I want."

He kissed me softly before he wiped the tears and rain from my cheeks. He saw.

Alice VL

I DO (NOT) – ON ICE

"So, are you saying we should just pass each other in corridors and elevators like strangers?"

It was a terrible idea. My heart missed a beat, and then another one. I could feel the shudders inside of me by the sheer thought of pretending that Daniel, my fireman was no longer an imbedded fragment of my life. I hated to admit it, but it stung more than it should have.

"Yes."

He retreated slightly before he turned around and walked away from me. I watched him walk away but was tempted to run after him. I didn't understand my emotions. I was frantic to convince myself that I hadn't fallen in love with him. Or had I?

'No, no, no.'

I didn't love Daniel Sotherby. Never. Not in a million years. I could never fall in love again. I liked him. I owed him my liberation. I owed him the first of many highs. I owed him everything physical, but, I didn't love him. This was my life. This was what I wanted.

I turned back to my car and slid into the driver's seat.

'This is what I want.'

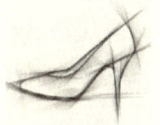

Alice VL

I DO (NOT) – ON ICE

I staggered into my apartment shortly after eight. It was dark, and the rain was not about to let up any time soon. I was haunted by Daniel's words and I couldn't get the sorrowful look on Daniel's face off my mind. I still felt awful. I couldn't shake the feeling that I had betrayed him.

'I need a warm bath.'

While waiting for the water to fill my bath tub, I sat on the edge and turned my attention back to William. My encounter with the fancy doctor was nothing short of wonderful. Amazing. Different than with Daniel, almost better. But, it was quick, unlike with Daniel, and in all fairness, it was our very first encounter. No judgements yet.

I was determined to brush off the confrontation with Daniel, and focused solely on the good doctor. I was excited to see William again, but more than that, I was desperate to put Daniel behind me. I didn't like feeling vulnerable and I didn't like feeling as though a shard of glass had been thrust into my heart.

I quickly placed my mobile on the side of the bath before I climbed in. The water was warm and comforting, so I laid back and listened to the rain come crashing down on the roof. I closed my eyes and indulged in the sounds the raindrops made as they hit the ground. It pacified and calmed me. For a moment, I thought of nothing else than the rain flooding the roads outside.

My mind wandered off to William. He was almost disconcertingly gentle. Tender. Caring. Again, I compared him to Daniel. He was passionate. Determined. Loving.

'Why the hell am I comparing the two?'

Alice VL

I DO (NOT) – ON ICE

I once again berated myself for reflecting on Daniel and our extraordinary encounters. Still, each time I closed my eyes, his eyes come back to haunt me. There was a sadness I had never seen before in any man and it made me feel insecure.

I was ruffled and wholly unprepared for the way it made me feel, but, I reminded myself that I had never been one to witness someone else's hurt. It always negatively affected me. It would infiltrate me every single time. Whether or not I was intimately connected to someone, I took no pleasure in another's pain.

'That's all it is, Ally. You like William. You like Doctor William Walker. You do not want to see Daniel again.'

As I attempted to convince myself, my phone rang out of the blue, jolting me back to reality at once. I was startled and sat up straight. I clutched my mobile phone and recognized my father's number on the screen. I was without a shadow of a doubt, not in the mood to speak to my parents, least of all my father. Yet, ignoring his call would just make him more determined to get a hold of me. He would never stop calling.

"Ally here."

"Ally Bradshaw!"

By his abrupt tone, I detected the undoubted exasperation in my dad's voice. He was irritated and quite possibly fuming.

'What did I do?'

"Hi dad."

Alice VL

I DO (NOT) – ON ICE

"Don't you 'hi' me, Ally Bradshaw."

"What's going on? What did I do?"

"Your mother and I am so disappointed in you."

'Oh Lord'. My mom was on the other extension and just had to deal me the disappointment card.

'What the hell did I do?'

"Hi mom."

"Michael called us. He is worried about you and thinks you need help."

I burst out laughing, but bravely attempted to hide my amusement from my parents.

'Seriously? Did Michael actually call my parents and complain? I wonder what he told them?'

"Really? You are listening to Michael? What did he say?"

"He says you asked him to come over and drugged him by spiking his coffee. He says when he woke up, he was on your bed, blindfolded, tied and naked and that you apparently called Lily?"

I could hear the utter disgust in my mother's voice.

'What a total ass.'

"Is that what he said?"

"How could you stoop so low, Ally? He made a mistake

Alice VL

when he wandered off, but you should've found it in your heart to forgive him. But no, what do you do? You divorce him. And now that he's happy again, you try to sabotage that too?"

My dad had made up his mind. I couldn't believe that Michael lied to them and I could just speculate on what it was he said to Lily. 'I did not see this coming.' Michael was quick on his feet. He was a salesman after all, but this was a whole new kind of low, even for him.

"You know, mom and dad. I did do that. Damn right I did! I would do it again. But I didn't drug him. I didn't even ask him over. He never leaves me alone and constantly messages me or shows up at the museum. I wanted to teach him a lesson and I wanted him to leave me alone!"

"Yes, he said you'd say that!"

'Are you kidding?'

"Why do you think that is, mom? Because it's the truth!"

"Your mother and I have talked it over and we are of the opinion that you come home when you take your annual leave in June. We will try and get you the help you need."

'Wait. Hang on.' My dad expected me to spend three weeks in Water Hill, Constantia? With them? That was not going to happen.

"I'll come for a few days, but I am definitely not going down for three weeks."

"That's up to you. We'll just come visit you and get you

the help you need there."

'No. Hell no.' I did not want my parents here for three weeks. I let out an enormous sigh, one I was sure they could hear. There was no changing their minds. I would simply have to suck it up and go down to Constantia. I had no choice. My parents are vicious.

'Screw you, Michael'.

"Fine!"

"Good. So, we'll see you in June. And don't worry honey … everything will be okay."

"Everything is okay, mom."

I didn't hear my father again, and when my mom finally ended the call, I laid back and slipped down below the surface of the water.

'What a shitty day.' I was instantly irritated and by the time I climbed out the bath, I was not only angry, but shaken. I reached for my mobile phone without drying myself off, and typed out a hurried message to Michael,

'Fuck you, Michael Bradshaw. This must be a new kind of low even for you to call my parents. You are a sorry excuse and you know what else? Your dick is ugly. Revolting. Small. Pathetic. Old. Limp. Dry. Inexperienced. Unfulfilling. I have had better sex in two weeks than I have had in an entire lifetime with you. Just so you know, it is awful to be screwed by a corpse?'

I wrapped the towel around me and slipped in under the

Alice VL

covers. I was just about to turn on the television when I heard the bleeping of my phone,

'Ally. You need help. Your parents will take care of you. What you did to Michael was really mean and completely out of character. I can't believe you'd stoop so low as to drug him and practically rape him. Then you call me and try to frame him? Don't take your anger out on Michael. He doesn't love you anymore. He doesn't want you. Listen to your parents and get help. Lily.'

I was fuming. Livid. I could kill her and had she been standing in front of me, I probably would bash her face in. 'Oh, screw you, Lily. Are you just as big an idiot as he is? I actually felt sorry for you when I called you. Now I just think you're stupid. Believe what you like and tell Michael to leave me alone!'

I needed to calm down. I needed to find something to distract me. 'Why does it feel like everything is crashing down on me and falling apart around me?' I didn't want to call Bianca and I don't know William well enough; I certainly didn't want to speak to Daniel.

Instead of reaching out to any of them, I tossed my phone onto my bed and crawled in under the covers. I wanted to run away and hide. I wished with all my heart I had never met or married Michael. I wished I never had met or fallen in lust with Daniel. I wished I was still with William, in his apartment.

Alice VL

I DO (NOT) – ON ICE

PART 4

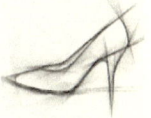

'I can't believe its Monday already!'

I dragged myself out of bed and couldn't stop reflecting on the events of the weekend and how my own game drastically backfired on me and shot me in the foot.

I didn't sleep a wink and found myself replaying my conversation with Daniel repeatedly. I didn't understand my emotions and by the time I climbed out of the shower, I made a firm decision to recover from the unwanted feelings I had for him. I was determined to shove Daniel to the back of my mind, and to discard all the haunting emotions running wild inside of me.

I smiled when I thought of William. He was poles apart from Daniel. He was clean-shaven, had soft hands and was gentler. A true gentleman. I thought of Michael. Asshole. Backstabber.

By the time I walked through the large wooden doors of the museum, I was irritable and exhausted. I walked from room to room switching on the lights, but that morning, I didn't stop off at Anne-Marie's painting. I was mad at her, yet, I was not sure why.

I DO (NOT) – ON ICE

When I finally reached my office, I quickly slid my bag in under my desk and when I pulled out my mobile phone, I noticed two text messages. One was from Bianca and the other from Daniel.

'So, how did it go'"

"If only you knew." I whispered softly.

Bianca was my only happy place at that very moment, and I couldn't help but snuffle slightly when I read her message.

'Great! And then not so great …'

'What happened?'

'Daniel. Michael. My parents.'

'Oh shit. Do you want to talk?'

'Can you come over tonight?'

'Sure. Should I bring food?'

'Lots.'

'Okay hon … chin up. See you tonight.'

I scrolled down to the next message. My heart hammered instantly, as though it was about to jump right out of my chest.

'Ally. I am sorry. I really want to be able to say hi when I see you. I don't want this, whatever this is. Let's just be able to say hi and bye, please.'

Alice VL

I DO (NOT) – ON ICE

My heart hurt. Again. And again, I could in no way at all, identify my feelings.

'I am sorry too. You are such a great guy, Daniel. I want nothing more than for us to be friends. I mean it.'

I hit send and sat back in my chair. I waited. There was no further response. I pulled out William's business card and immediately typed out a text to him. I needed distraction. I needed a friendly text.

'Thank you for yesterday.'

Again, I hit send and waited. Barely a minute later, a bleeping sound came through,

'I had a great evening. Can we do it again?'

Aah. Just what I needed to snap out of my foul mood.

'I'll call you.' I really wanted to see William Walker again.

"Can't wait."

Again, no request for a phone number or address. I was ecstatic.

'Oh, Ally you idiot. He has your number from your text message.'

"Right."

An hour before the museum was to close, I quickly dialed the consulting rooms of Doctor Richard Hanson.

"Doctor Hanson's office."

"Hi. I'd like to schedule a consultation with Doctor Walker please."

"What for?"

'How rude!'

For a second, I was taken aback. What a cow. I was convinced that she was one of those stuck-up, suit-wearing, middle-aged, man-less and grumpy women that some of my snobbish school friends turned into.

"That's why I need a consultation."

"But for what? Liposuction? A nose job? A breast enlargement? Vaginal restoration?"

'Hang on. What?'

"Vaginal restoration?"

I heard an undeniable, irritable sigh,

"That's when your vagina gets tightened again. It's very popular in women who go through natural childbirth. Or would you prefer the virginity restorer?"

'Are you kidding? Did she just ask me if I wanted my virginity restored?'

"Sorry, what?"

Another sigh. She was growing increasingly frustrated by

my obvious ignorance.

"We can give you your virginity back. Yes."

I giggled softly and wasn't sure if she was mocking me or if that was actually a thing. I had never before heard of such a procedure and I was shocked.

'Seriously? Women do that? Why?'

"I would simply like a consultation on a breast lift."

She was silent. I knew instinctively that she was irritated by me.

"Doctor Walker may not be able to assist but I can squeeze you in on Tuesday at 3pm or 6pm for a consultation."

"Tuesday as in tomorrow?"

"Yes, as in tomorrow. There are two cancellations. The next available appointment is in three weeks."

"6pm then?"

"Name?"

"Ally Bradshaw."

"Age."

"Really?"

"Oh Lord. Yes really."

'What is this bitch's problem?'

I DO (NOT) – ON ICE

"Thirty-one."

"Phone number."

I quickly gave her my phone number and immediately regretted my decision.

"Alright Mrs. Bradshaw. Tomorrow at 6pm."

"Thank you. It's Miss. You are?"

"Brenda Colt. Office Manager."

'Aah, that makes sense. She's probably just filling in for the receptionist.'

"Thank you."

Without acknowledging or responding to me, Brenda Colt ended the call almost as abruptly as what our entire conversation was. 'No, you're welcome?'

I locked up the museum a short while later and headed out back to my apartment, hoping desperately that Bianca did not show up late. I was starving. When I reached the front door of my apartment, I was at once happy to see her standing there, carrying copious amounts of junk food.

"I didn't know what you wanted, so I got a little bit of everything. Here's fish, chicken, beef, burgers, pasta and ice-cream."

She lifted the bags to me and my mood was elevated at once.

I DO (NOT) – ON ICE

"You are such a good friend."

After unlocking my front door, I took a few bags from her and together, we made our way into the kitchen. After placing the bags on the counter, I took out two dinner plates and two wine glasses. I slid a plate over to her and took out a bottle of wine from the fridge.

After filling both glasses, I gulped down mine and refilled it straight away.

"Wow. Rough day?"

Bianca watched me with caution as I took another large sip of my refilled wine glass.

"You have no idea."

I plonked myself onto a kitchen stool across from her and begin unpacking the fast food bags. After filling my plate with chicken, calamari and French fries, I turned back to her.

"So, after you left William's place, we of course … did it."

"I figured as much. How was it?"

"It was great. I want to say better than Daniel, but I'm not sure that's the right word. Different. But quick. I think it was really too quick but, it was our first time."

Bianca almost choked as she bit into a hamburger.

"So, I left … which was so uncomplicated. He didn't insist on a phone number, address or anything like that, but guess who I run into in the elevator?"

Alice VL

I DO (NOT) – ON ICE

"Uh oh!"

"Daniel. And he was pissed. And by then, it had started to rain. He was on his way to work, but followed me to my car ... it was awful."

"Awful how?"

"He was disgusted with me. Disappointed. I don't think I'll ever forget that look in his eyes. It was horrible, Bianca!"

"What did he say?"

"That's the thing, I can barely remember what he said. But, I can't forget the look in his eyes. He was hurt and let down. He knew I was with someone ... he just knew."

"He's fallen for you."

"I don't even know how to respond to that."

"Listen honey ..."

Bianca placed her hamburger on her plate and had a sip of her wine,

"I think you've fallen for him too ..."

I was horrified by Bianca's accusation. It was so not true. Wrong. Inaccurate. She was way off the mark.

"I didn't fall for him, Bianca. I am not falling for him now. I feel bad and I feel like I owe him."

"For what?"

I DO (NOT) – ON ICE

"For ... you know? I didn't want to hurt him. We had a wonderful few weeks and I don't want to remember it as something horrible. Something I never should have done."

"Don't worry about it, Ally. These things sort themselves out. So, are you seeing William again?"

"Yep. I have an appointment for tomorrow, 6pm."

"Are you kidding?"

"Nope!"

"We both burst out laughing and tucked back into our food.

"Oh shit, I almost forgot?"

"What?"

"My parents called yesterday."

"Uh oh!"

"Guess what Michael did? He called my dad and told him that I drugged him, tied him up, blindfolded him, got him naked and left him before calling Lily to come pick him up. Basically, I framed him."

"Are you shitting me? Drugged him?"

"Yep. And my dad believes every word. As does my mom."

"I wonder what Lily thinks?"

Alice VL

I DO (NOT) – ON ICE

"I sent Michael a hate text yesterday, and she replied saying that I needed help."

"Holy shit! Are you serious? That girl needs to open her eyes!"

I reached for the ice-cream and grabbed a spoon all at the same time.

"So anyway, my parents insist that I use my leave days and go out to Constantia for the entire three weeks so that they can get me the supposed help I need."

"Are you?"

"I have no choice. You know my parents. They'd just pitch up and not leave again, so yes. I'll go. I just don't want to."

"Michael is such a twat."

"I told him his manhood was ugly, limp and old."

Bianca erupted into violent laughter, almost choking on her food before she spat it all out. I laughed out loud and was suddenly enormously proud of myself. Through all that was going on in my life at that very moment, at least I was having sex. Hot, steamy and well-endowed sex.

Bianca left just before midnight, after we both polished two bottles of wine. When she left, my mood was lifted and after a quick bath, I climbed into bed and fell asleep almost straight away. It was a bad day. But, it was a good day too.

The following morning and to my surprise, I woke up

Alice VL

I DO (NOT) – ON ICE

early and in a much better mood. I carefully chose a loose fitting, flowing dress and a pair of heels to match. I was feeling particularly sensual and I was convinced that nothing could spoil my mood.

My work day flew by but again, I didn't stop by Anne-Marie. I was angry with her, for no apparent reason at all. I was still rattled by Daniel's behavior and I could barely rid myself of his rousing fragrance. For some reason, Anne-Marie reminded me of my mortal sin against my fireman.

At five minutes to six, I strolled into the consultation rooms of Doctor Richard Hanson as gracefully as I could. I walked over to the front office reception desk, faking confidence and grace. When I heard her speak, I instantly recognized the voice as that of Brenda Colt.

"Mrs. Bradshaw?"

"Yes, that's me. But it's Miss."

"Please complete this form and hand it back to me when you're done."

I took the stack of forms from her, before I snatched a clipboard and pen from the counter. I sat down and quickly completed what felt to me like an examination paper.

Every aspect of my life was questioned; from my parents, right down to me. I ticked mostly 'no' but when I see that question, it stopped me dead in my tracks,

'Have you had more than one sexual partner in the last six months?'

Alice VL

I DO (NOT) – ON ICE

Seriously, they give you a measly six months? 'Shit.'

I don't know how to answer. I didn't want to lie, but at the same time, I wasn't comfortable to tell the truth either. I was not in the mood for Brenda Colt's accusatory stares.

'Let me lie ... I'm not going through with it anyways.'

I tick off no and was quite pleased and comfortable with my answer. I handed her back the forms and made my way back to my seat.

"Where are you going?"

I stared at her and again.

I didn't really know how to answer her. She scared me a little.

"Back to my seat?"

"No, you're not. Follow me."

I quickly picked up my bag and followed closely behind her.

'What I don't put up with for good, mind-blowing and earth-shattering encounters with Doctor William Walker.'

She showed me into an office and pointed to an empty seat.

"Wait here. Doctor Walker will be in shortly."

"Thanks."

Alice VL

I DO (NOT) – ON ICE

I sat down. I was nervous. Wary. I didn't trust Brenda Colt at all. I placed my bag beneath my chair and glanced around me. It was all extremely clinical and clean. I hated doctors' rooms. I hated hospitals. I just hated everything about that environment.

While still scrutinizing my surroundings, the door opened again and in walked the doctor. By the look on his face, I could at once detect his surprise, but at the same time, he was happy to see me.

"Ally?"

"I told you I wanted a consultation."

"I told you, you didn't need one."

"Well, maybe I just want you to feel me up again."

He grinned from ear to before he latched the office door behind him. I got up and walked over to him.

"Actually, Doctor Walker, I'm not feeling well at all."

"Oh?"

"I have this deep unsettling sensation somewhere in the area of my thighs, and I've heard a vaginal regeneration might do the trick. Apparently, you can do that these days?"

'Good grief, Ally!'

I slipped my arms around his neck and pressed myself firmly against him.

"Also, my chest hurts when I think of going to the doctor.

Alice VL

Is that normal?"

"I can't diagnose you like this. I'd have to examine you thoroughly."

"Oh, I so hoped you would say that."

'Oh my word! Who have I become? I am scaring myself a little.'

I immediately shoved him into a wall, and anxiously removed his white, intimidating doctor's coat. Underneath, he was wearing a buttoned shirt, tie and jeans. I grinned. I liked the combination and impatiently unzipped his jeans.

My hands trailed down, desperate to catch a glimpse of his secret weapon. I slowly emancipated him from his jeans, and again, no underwear.

'I like this man.'

When I finally was able to catch that ever-evasive glimpse, I was pleasantly surprised, although a little shocked; they are certainly not all the same. Again, it was a never-seen before moment for me. I was instantly persuaded that I had never seen anything as overpowering as what I was seeing in that consulting room. Then again, I had not seen much of anything in my life.

I was in lust. Again. I was thrilled to be in the presence of another masterpiece. I placed my arms around him and squeezed him firmly, almost to acknowledge my approval and to thank him for his magnificence.

He was still totally dissimilar to Daniel, but still a

masterpiece of a man.

I pressed my lips onto his and pushed myself firmly against him. William placed his arms around me and pushed himself as close to him as he could.

"Shit."

He began grunting loudly before he picked me up and placed me on his examination bed.

"Oh, Doctor Walker ..."

"You are a very ill patient ..."

I sat up straight and when he fell to his knees, I could barely contain my excitement.

'Oh Lord.'

His lips moved over my thighs as he made his way up over my entire body until he reached my mouth. With his tongue searching mine, he sent shivers down my spine. The warmth of his mouth was surprisingly stimulating and I couldn't help but notice how his tongue felt enormous, rigid and fleshy.

He withdrew slightly and began carving at my neck while sliding his arms in under me, pulling me up against him. The shudders I was beginning to know so well were once again, running up and down my spine. A new kind of jolt, one I have never known before settled and delighted me from the inside out.

Again, I was introduced to vibrations I had never known

I DO (NOT) – ON ICE

before. He moved slowly and when he finally pressed against me, a sudden but familiar pulsating began to engulf and wholly overwhelm me.

I tried to push him away, but it was too late. My body began erupting into one enormous disturbance as my legs broke out into a severe quake. My knees trembled underneath his hands as he tightened his grip on them when they instinctively tried to close.

He didn't stop, not even for a moment. Instead, he moved slowly, but firmly. There was no muffling any sound coming from my mouth. I didn't want to. I didn't even try to.

When he pulled me closer to him, I lifted myself up and leaned on my hands behind me. Instinctively, I wrapped my legs around him, and pulled him even closer. William grabbed onto my thighs and at once, he began to seize fiercely.

While my entire body once again lost all control, I stared blankly at him and was instantly and intensely aware of the build-up of sensuality. When he again tightened his hands on my thighs, I grabbed onto his arms and held on for dear life.

Brenda Colt suddenly came to mind and I desperately tried to hold my breath. I was frantic to muffle the chaotic noises that emanated from us both, and held my breath once again. Within seconds, every sensation, each tremble and every single burst inside of me, spurted from my mouth. William shuddered shortly after while digging his fingers into my thighs before he lowered his head. His breaths were almost labored while I leaned back, equally breathless.

Alice VL

I gasped for air when he retreated slightly while still moaning softly. He lifted his eyes and stared at me unable to hide a sneaky grin that was slowly growing broader.

"I think your treatment has been administered. You should be fine but if your condition persists, please call me. You might require additional treatments to be sure. I still do house-calls just in case you were wondering."

"Oh, Doctor Walker, I actually do feel so much better. Thank you. Not quite cured, but definitely better."

He recoiled just enough to zip his jeans. I climbed off the bed and straightened my flowing dress.

'Thank God for these dresses.'

William gallantly walked over to the other side of his desk and casually slid into his chair, still panting slightly.

"So, Miss Bradshaw. As I've said before, I see no need for a breast enlargement or lift for that matter."

"I will most certainly take your advice under consideration although I don't necessarily agree."

When I heard his amusing chuckle, I smirked and lowered my head. I was once again taken aback by his striking, seductive smile.

"Thank you again."

"You're very welcome."

When I reached his door, I quickly unlatched it and

turned back one more time.

"Bye, Doc."

"Bye."

Shutting the door firmly behind me, I made my way down the corridor and through the reception area. I didn't want to make eye contact with Brenda or listen to her judgmental tone. As I was about to leave the consulting offices, I heard her call out behind me.

'Oh Lord.' I tensed up at once.

"Mrs. Bradshaw!"

I was not in the mood to correct her on my Miss'ness again and sighed.

"Yes?"

I turned around, my head slightly bowed. I was truly not in the mood for her.

"Do we need to schedule a follow up appointment?"

"No. I have decided against the surgery."

"Are you sure?"

She was staring at my chest and the disapproval on her face was evident, leaving me feeling self-conscious almost at once. 'What a cheek! Cow.'

"Why? Do you think I need an enlargement?"

I DO (NOT) – ON ICE

"Well, there is always room for improvement."

'Are you kidding me?' This woman was working on my last nerve. I wanted to walk up to her and smack her right across her face, while wiping that sarcastic grin right from her mouth. But, I didn't. I sneered instead.

"Doctor Walker thinks the procedure is completely unnecessary, so … I won't be going ahead with it."

Her sarcastic, mocking smile turned into a frown at once. I smiled, my small toe began curling up as I studied her face and tried to identify the expression in her eyes. Without saying another word, she turned around and disappeared behind her counter.

"Thank God …"

I turned around and quickly made my way to my car.

'What a total bitch.'

Just as I slid into the driver's seat, I heard a familiar bleeping on my phone.

'I need to find a less irritating tone for this damn phone.' I mumbled while scrolling down my messages.

'How was it?'

It was Bianca. She probably sat timing me from the moment my appointment began. I laughed out loudly.

'Instead of breast enlargement surgery, I opted for an injection. I feel great!'

Alice VL

I DO (NOT) – ON ICE

'Oh Lord, Ally Bradshaw. You are turning into a man-monster.'

'That I sure am!'

After going back and forth for a while, I tossed my phone into my bag and drove off, back to my apartment. I was exhausted, and it was only Tuesday. Without intending to, I slowly passed by the mall, hoping to catch a glimpse of Daniel, even though I knew that the chance of seeing him was extremely slim. I had no idea what his schedule was like. I had lost track of his shifts, and I didn't have a clue whether he was in fact working, or on rest days. When I turned the corner, I couldn't believe my luck when I caught a glimpse of him walking out, fully dressed and equipped for work. He took my breath away and rather than admitting it to myself, I kept myself safely hidden behind invisible barricades I had created for one reason only; to keep me single and sane.

I pulled into a parking spot and after I switched my car off, I sat staring at him. Again, I didn't understand my sudden and unanticipated obsession with Daniel. I had been perfectly fine for the two weeks after my last meeting with him, but all I could do at that very second, was think about Daniel, my fireman.

I watched him walk over to his truck and when he climbed into his driver's seat, my heart sank. I became instantly aware of a glazed, glassy layer of tears sting in my eyes and when I blinked, they dropped from my eyelids and onto my cheeks. Daniel weighed heavily on me and I could in no way at all, make sense of what I was feeling or why a wretched kind of sadness, another first for me, had made its way into the very core of me.

Alice VL

I DO (NOT) – ON ICE

Losing Max all those years ago, left me with a kind of sadness I thought I could never feel again. It left me devastated and in a daze, as though my heart had been ripped out of me, shattered into a million pieces, and then propped back into my body. It was a kind sorrow I couldn't put out into words, but one I truly believed I would never have to live through again. Often, memories of him would remind me of the aftermath of those emotions and at the same time, the wretchedness would in turn, create more memories of pain, hurt and desolation.

"Did I make a mistake?"

I couldn't help but question my emotions while desperately trying to decipher the unbearable grief I was feeling. I couldn't banish the expression in his eyes from my mind; the way he looked at me while the rain came crashing down on us. I felt a faint jab rush through my heart and settle into my stomach. I felt sick.

It hurt, so much and I didn't like the way he made me feel anymore. It felt as though I didn't know anything anymore. The silence around me was deafening and I couldn't quite translate or untangle any of my emotions.

Instead, I did what I always do. I made a conscious decision to put him behind me and forced my mind and my common sense back to William Walker and my encounters with him. Those same butterflies that caused me pain only a few days ago, were back, and fluttering stronger and more powerful than ever before, just as they should be.

'Stop, Ally. Your mind is playing tricks on you. Forget Daniel.'

Alice VL

I DO (NOT) – ON ICE

"Daniel who?"

I was convinced and satisfied that Daniel was nothing more than the man who found me on a day I was most vulnerable. He took pity on me when he flung me into a world of sensations and sizzles; a kind of a world that I had only ever heard of. Because of that, he was special and because of that, I knew that I would always feel more drawn to Daniel than anyone else.

He made it real for me. He made me his queen and his kitchen stool was my throne. When Daniel pulled away, I pulled up behind him before he turned left at the intersection. I turned right. Just as it should be.

When I reached my apartment less than ten minutes later, I hastily ran a warm bath and lay soaking in it for almost an hour. Each time I closed my eyes, I made a concerted effort to think of no-one else, but of William.

Glimpses of Daniel kept threatening to overpower my thoughts, but after rudely scolding my mind, it was William's frosty eyes that ultimately won out.

I climbed into bed after a quick sandwich and a hot cup of coffee. After watching television for about an hour, I took my mobile phone and messaged Daniel, against my better judgement. Against all the scoldings and warnings between my mind and my heart, I just couldn't escape him.

'Be safe tonight.'

After staring at my screen for a few minutes longer, I relented and placed my mobile phone on my bedside table and fell asleep almost at once.

I dreamed of Daniel and then, I dreamed of William. At one point during these nightmarish hallucinations, I woke up with a hammering heart, desperate to catch my breath. I woke up terrified when I found myself dead in the center of them both in a wild, raunchy and compromising position.

I cringed often, upset by the delusions that were slowly invading every part of me. I may be Ally Bradshaw, but I was not that brave. I could ever venture over to the other side; like Bianca would say, 'to the darkest side of sex.' No. For now, it was William and William alone. I could not, for the life of me, even understand why I had dreamed such crap.

When I woke up the following morning, I was once again forced to drag myself out of bed. I stood under the shower and as though in a wandering haze, I washed and conditioned my hair without paying attention to much of anything around me.

While viciously brushing my teeth, I stared at the tired, drawn and sorrowful looking redhead staring back at me.

'Don't lose focus, Ally. Do not let Daniel steal your individualism, liberation or joy.'

After dressing for work, I quickly gulped down a cup of coffee and grabbed my mobile phone.

"I didn't even see a message ..."

I frowned when I noticed one new message and scrolled down,

'Thanks, Ally. I miss you ...'

My heart broke out into a thousand flutters, but felt as though a sharp dagger was jabbing at me, all at the same time. I didn't reply. I didn't want to. I did, but I didn't. At that very instant, I didn't know what I wanted. Daniel was wholly infiltrating and overpowering my mind, but worse, he was muddying my heart.

I didn't want to surrender to any of what I was feeling. I didn't want to be trapped by one man again, ever. My focus now was on William, at least, until he leaves to head back to Sutherland which turned out to be two days before I leave for Constantia.

'No more Daniel. No more messages to Daniel. No stalking Daniel. Nothing Daniel.'

I had to repeat those words over and over again, and by the time I reached the museum, I had almost persuaded myself.

I walked slowly through the museum as I picked up my early morning routine. When I reached Anne-Marie's painting, I stood still; something I hadn't done in a while.

"Actually, Anne-Marie. You got what you deserved. We all do, eventually."

Even to myself, I sounded bitter. Angry. I was slowly evolving from feelings of liberation and fun to feeling trapped and miserable. I didn't understand my sentiments and Anne-Marie staring back at me, wasn't helping me one bit.

I marched into my office and when Gill pitched up ten

minutes late, I snapped at her,

"Gill. This is the last time you march in here late. Expect a written warning the next time."

I had never reprimanded any of my employees for showing up late to work. I had never been that kind of a manager and I once swore, never to become that kind of person. It never worried me before, but today was different. I felt undermined and disrespected. I felt as though my staff were taking advantage of me due to my lack of rule enforcement.

"I'm sorry Ally. My ride was late."

"Next time, have the decency to call me, and let me know."

I turned around and made a mad dash for my office. I already felt wicked and evil and I was convinced that I was a horrible person. I realized as I closed my office door behind me, it was not the fact that Gill was late that bothered me, I troubled me. Ally bothers Ally.

Barely ten minutes later, Gill walked in and placed a warm cup of coffee on my desk.

"Thank you, Gill. Did I ask you for coffee?"

"No, you didn't, but you've never shouted at me before and I just figured … you need that cup of coffee."

"Thank you. I'm sorry. From the bottom of my heart, I regret snapping at you. I know you depend on rides to get to work. Please accept my apologies."

Alice VL

I DO (NOT) – ON ICE

"You're welcome and no apology necessary, Ally."

I kept myself locked up and hidden in my office for the remainder of the day. My thoughts were twisting and turning almost choking me with their whispers. At one point, they became torturous and tormented my feelings for Daniel.

When the last of the staff left for the day, I emerged from my office for the first time. I was too ashamed to face Gill after my outburst. It was a bad day. All I could think of was, that bloody fireman.

Only ten minutes before, did I switch off the lights of the museum when the large wooden doors opened again. My heart nearly missed a beat and I was certain that my eyes are playing tricks on me.

'Oh no. It's Daniel.'

"Daniel?"

"Hey … I swear, I am just here to check the fire extinguishers. For no other reason. I didn't want to come out here but my Captain insisted and I didn't quite know what to say. I am not here to unsettle you, Ally."

"You can never unsettle me, Daniel. Do you know where the extinguishers are? I'll switch the lights back on."

'Karma. You bitch.'

"Two should be over there …"

He pointed towards the end of the museum when he

spotted them straight away, and swiftly marched over to them while I hurriedly switched on the lights. One by one, he picked each one up and placed a new sticker around them.

When he was satisfied that they were both in good working order, he walked back over to me.

"According to my paperwork, one should be in your office?"

"Oh? I've never really noticed?"

"It should be behind your door?"

"Okay. Well, let's go look."

When we reached my office, we both walked in. Daniel closed the door behind him and we both noticed the fire extinguisher at the same time.

"If that was a snake ..."

"You can be glad it's not." Daniel chuckled almost inaudibly.

He checked each nozzle and tested the pressure before placing a brand-new sticker around it and fitted it back onto the wall bracket.

"That should be good for another six months."

I quickly opened my door and was beginning to feel uncomfortable and entirely out of place. I couldn't stand the smell of his cologne suddenly; I felt sick to my stomach. It drew me in, stupefied me and made me sick all at the same time. I abruptly walked out and Daniel followed me without saying a word.

When we reached the front doors of the museum, he stopped and turned to face me. He stared at me for what felt like forever, but he didn't say a word.

"Thanks for stopping by … and checking the fire extinguishers …"

"You're welcome, but honestly, I was just doing my job. But at the same time, I must admit that it was good seeing you again."

"Thank you, Danny …"

I wanted to place my arms around his neck and kiss him. Nothing more. No sex. No high. I just wanted to kiss him. I wanted him to sweep me up and hold me. Just that. Kiss me and hold me. I was losing my mind. I had this. For twelve years, I was stuck with a desperate need to be held and kissed until I no longer wanted that.

I didn't want that anymore so why was it all I could think of? Daniel pulled me closer and embraced me warmly. I rested my head against his chest and breathed him in again. I listened to the sound of his beating heart and it soothed me. It appeased me almost at once. I fitted perfectly in his arms and I liked it there.

Instinctively, I placed my arms around him and held him equally snugly against me. It felt as though he was sheltering me from a world that was beginning to betray me. He was familiar to my heart. As I rested my head against him, I realized with shock that he felt like home.

I withdrew slightly, overcome with feelings of chaos and turmoil growing inside of me. I couldn't make head or tails of my emotions as I looked into his eyes and tried to understand what was going on with me.

"Daniel ... I'm ... I'm kinda seeing someone."

"No, you're not, Ally. You're having sex, but you're not seeing anyone."

He was right. How can this fireman be so smart?

"So anyways ... I better be off. Please let me know if there are any problems with the extinguishers, okay?"

"Okay. Wait. Daniel?"

"Yep?"

I wanted to tell him that my heart was fighting my mind for him. I wanted to ask him to wait for me; to be patient. I wanted to tell him that he felt like home and that I was pretty sure I would eventually come home, but for now, my insides were jumbled, muddied and tangled. I didn't understand, no matter how hard I tried. Instead, I stuck to my plan,

"Be safe, okay?"

"You too, Ally."

When he walked out, I immediately shut the door behind him. I leaned against the door and breathed him in one more time. I couldn't get enough of this man or his smell. One moment he sickened me, but the next, he haunted me. I couldn't stop thinking about his skin against mine. Daniel Sotherby had a hold over me, and I didn't know how to break free from him.

Until I figured it all out, William Walker would just have to distract me. I was not prepared to go back to the kind of life I once had with Michael. I didn't want to be cheated on again. I didn't want to give my heart and soul away and trust just one person not to break it again.

'No.' I didn't want to invest in another man ever again in my life. I liked the moment I was living in, whatever that was. I liked that I could walk away with my heart intact. I liked the hunt. I liked the sensuality. I liked the fact that I could go home alone.

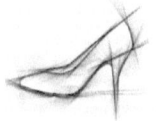

Alice VL

PART 5

For the next few weeks, I managed to avoid Daniel completely. I took the stairs up to the fourth floor each time I showed up at William's apartment, which was at least, two or three times a week.

William taught me new things about myself and swept me onto one high after another until Daniel began fading into the background. I no longer tried to analyze my feelings for him, and I managed to brush them off the moment they would flare up.

William never asked me for my address, and he never called my number, not even once. Bianca felt that it was a sign of detachment, but I didn't mind; I preferred it that way. At times, I would show up at his place wearing nothing but a coat. He would pull me into his apartment, and right there, my coat was ripped off, without either of us saying a word to one another.

When it was over, I would get up, slip my coat back on and walk away, back to my apartment and back to a life I had become obsessed with. It was how I liked it. It was baggage free and convenient. It was liberating and fulfilling. I wanted nothing more.

On the Monday morning before William was to return to his homelands, I made my rounds through the museum as I did each morning and after an entire weekend spent slipping in and out of William's apartment.

I was exhausted, yet exhilarated but I was in no way ready for Monday to begin. As I made my way to my office, I heard a knock on the museum doors. It was just after seven and the museum was only scheduled to open an hour later. I frowned, but hurried on over and quickly opened a single door. It was the good doctor.

"William?"

"Hi. I have a little time on my hands this morning. I've never been here before and just thought that before I go … to perhaps have a look around?"

"Sure. We open at eight so we're alone, and I'd love to show you around."

I stepped aside and locked the door behind him. William was casually dressed, clean-shaven and clean-smelling. I was not sure I could quite get used to his clinical appearance, or his equally austere smell. But damn, he was hot, handsome and blonde.

He glanced around in admiration,

"This place is great. I love the warmth of it. The wood, shaggy carpets, paintings and all things history."

"It is great. We have so much history dating back to hundreds of years and some will never truly understand the true value of it."

He turned around and smiled,

I DO (NOT) – ON ICE

"So, take me on a tour …"

I brushed past him and grabbed his hand. We walked through the narrow passage that led out to the room at the end of the hall. 'Anne-Marie's room.' When we stepped inside, William was stunned and strolled over to all the showcases displaying what I like to call, historical treasures.

One by one, he inspected each item and read up on each of them. He appeared just as a little boy in a toy store who was extremely excited, and continued to glance around in admiration.

I walked over to Anne-Marie and stared at her. She was a beautiful woman. There was a sadness in her eyes that would often haunt me. It was a kind of wretchedness that would frighten and intimidate me on my off days.

She didn't deserve to have been married off to an old man, but more than anything, she didn't deserve to die at his hands. Only the day before, did I finally pick up the book, 'The Betrayal of Anne-Marie Cromwell.' I was horrified to discover the true depths of her torture.

I couldn't take my eyes off her as I tried to imagine the pain and suffering she must have endured. When I felt William's warm breath on my neck, I was suddenly jolted back to reality. Still standing behind me, he wrapped his arms around me and gently kissed my neck.

"Who's that beaut?

"Anne-Marie Cromwell."

Alice VL

I DO (NOT) – ON ICE

He lifted his head slightly and frowned,

"Who?"

"A young girl whose parents married her off to a much older, but wealthy business man. Basically, he bought her from them. She fell hopelessly in love with a man named Amos and met him on the sly as often as she could. When Donald found out about it, he had Amos brought to their bedroom where he made him watch as he raped and beat Anne-Marie within inches of her life. When he was finished with her, he walked out and left her to die in Amos' arms."

"Shit Ally. I wish I never asked."

His one hand began trailing upwards while his other hand clutched at my belly before he kissed me ever so gently. His lips were soft and they carefully made their way down to my shoulder. I lean backwards when his arms folded around me.

Unlike most other days, I was dressed in an elegant, grey pants suit and a white blouse. My hair was neatly pulled back, but my heels were almost certainly higher than my standards.

When I turned around to face him, he clutched my face with his hands and kissed me again. I instinctively reached for his zipper and unzipped his trousers at once.

William stepped back and hurriedly undressed me from the waist down. When my clothes fell to the ground, he turned me around and pushed me up against a wall.

I was reeling. He pressed himself against me and began moving assertively at once. With my face and hands pressed against the wall, I pushed myself out slightly until he pressed firmly against me.

This was new to me. Different. It felt different. He moved quickly and when he grabbed my neck with one hand, I began to quiver ruthlessly. I could feel another kind of stimulating sensation I hadn't known until then. The sensual points were as though he was fervently rubbing against a shaft with a million tiny stimulating spots. My legs winced and my hands shuddered while my whimpering grew louder.

I could feel invigorating points send out electrifying shards up and down my spine.

I don't know this. I couldn't identify the sudden sensations that had unreservedly begun to incinerate me.

He pressed against me one more time, shoving me harder against the wall, leaving me unable to move. Each muscle in my body became rigid as my legs unexpectedly began to grow weak underneath me.

When William grabbed me around my waist and pulled me against him, I felt his body spasm almost at once. With one, soft mutter, he buried his head into my back and held onto me until it was all over.

When he stepped back, I turned to face him. I frowned and stared at the man who just sent me all the way onto cloud nine and pulled me back down at the speed of light. It was unlike anything I had ever felt before. It was intense, overwhelming but oh so quick.

Alice VL

I DO (NOT) – ON ICE

"You okay?"

When I quickly pulled up my trousers, I peered over at him and winked. I walked up to him and slid one hand around his neck, while my other hand gently touched his face.

"You were holding out on me, Doc."

I leaned in and kissed him, giving him my stamp of approval.

He smiled bashfully when I turned around and walked out of Anne-Marie's room,

"Goodbye, Doctor Walker. You can see yourself out."

"Goodbye Ally Bradshaw. Treatment must be working ..."

From the passage, I disappeared into the bathroom and quickly sponged myself down. I had ten minutes to pull myself together before the museum opened its doors.

When I heard the front door close, I smiled.

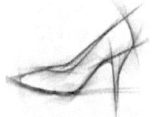

Alice VL

I DO (NOT) – ON ICE

On his last night in Willow County, I showed up at his apartment unannounced. I would normally send him a text and he would then respond with a time or an alternative day, depending on his commitments at the surgery. Being his last night in Willow County, I knew that he would be home, packing and getting ready to leave.

I went around the back and began climbing the stairs to the fourth floor. It was exhausting each time, and I was secretly relieved that William Walker, my raunchy doctor would be returning to his hometown soon.

When I reach number 411, I was surprised to find his door opened. I knocked softly, unsure if he had company, or if he simply neglected to close his front door.

I listened for voices and could clearly hear two voices coming closer. Before I could disappear down the hall; before I could accurately identify the second voice, Daniel was standing in front of me.

'Oh Lord.'

"Ally?"

"Hi ... Daniel ..."

I didn't know what to say. I didn't know how to respond. I wanted to disappear. Right there, I just wanted to vanish.

"You two know each other?"

Daniel smiled and turned around to face William,

I DO (NOT) – ON ICE

"Not personally. I've run into her at the museum. Bradshaw, right?"

He turned back to me, winked and smiled, this time at me.

'God, I love this man.'

I took his extended hand and shook it gently.

'No! I don't. I don't love this man!'

"I should be off."

"Thanks for stopping by, Daniel. I appreciate your help."

Daniel walked past me and disappeared out the front door almost as though he was being driven out by force. My heart sank at once, but I was intensely grateful to him for keeping our past a secret.

"Hi. I'm glad you came."

"What was he doing here?"

"Who? The fireman?"

"Yes."

"Oh. He was just servicing the extinguishers before I move out. Each tenant has to service it at the end of their contract term."

"You're kidding?"

"No. it comes off your security deposit if you don't."

Alice VL

"Wow! Never too old to learn!"

"So, are you going to stand there all night, or are you going to come inside?"

I stood quietly and stared. William Walker was an amazing man. Handsome. Successful. He possessed the ability undress my inner turmoil without any effort. His eyes were beautiful, his hands soft, but more than anything else, he had the broadest, most alluring smile I had ever seen.

But, he reeked of surgery and everything clinical. He had no odor. There was nothing intoxicating about him. I turned my head and scanned the passage behind me when I could still smell Daniel. I closed my eyes and breathed in his familiar forest, woody and rainy smell.

"I'm not coming in. I just wanted to stop by and say goodbye."

"You're not coming in?"

"No. I figured we should just say goodbye here. Now."

"That's a bummer."

He moved closer and placed his arms firmly around me. I breathed him in again. Nothing. No scent. No connection. Amazing sex. But nothing else.

"I am so glad I met you, Doctor William Walker."

"If ever you find yourself in Sutherland, you have my card."

I DO (NOT) – ON ICE

I kissed him tenderly and smiled.

"Goodbye William. Have a safe trip home."

"Goodbye Ally."

I turned around and walked away. I was relieved. I was going to miss the good doctor, but more than that, I wanted to see Daniel. I didn't want to fall for Daniel. I didn't. I just wanted to see him. Before I turned the corner, I looked back one last time.

William Walker was standing in the hallway, looking back at me. I stopped, turned around and waved and when he waved back, I carried on walking away from him.

When I reached the elevator, it felt as though I had reached some sort of crossroads in my life.

I didn't know which direction to take; up or down. Two floors up or four floors down.

'Two floors up or four floors down, Ally? Which will it be?'

When the doors opened, I step inside and hesitated. I didn't quite know what I was waiting for or what to listen for.

The doors closed and I realized that someone on another floor had probably pressed the elevator. It was going up. I passed the fifth floor, and wasn't sure whether I should hope for it to pass the sixth making its way all the way up to the twelfth floor. When number six came up, I was sure it was going to pass. It didn't. It stopped.

Alice VL

I DO (NOT) – ON ICE

The doors opened up suddenly and a young couple strolled in, hand in hand. I smiled and waited for the doors to close again. Just as the doors began to close, I pushed through and ran out. I was instantly flustered. My heart began to race. I could hear every single pound in my heart, drowning out any sounds around me and echoing throughout my entire body.

I had no idea what I was doing or how to explain myself to Daniel. I walked slowly. I always seemed to walk slowly on my way to Daniel's apartment.

When I reached his front door, I hesitated again. Without knocking, I turned around and began to walk away when I heard his front door open. I knew then that I had the worst luck in the world and if anybody had told me to look out for signs, that would be it.

"Ally?"

I stood still for a split-second before I turned around. I so desperately wanted to ask him to walk back in and un-see me at his front door.

"I ... I'm leaving for Constantia in two days for three weeks. I just wanted to say goodbye. I didn't want to say anything in front of William. By the way, thanks for that."

"You're leaving for Constantia?"

"It's a long story. Nothing important."

I swung my handbag from side to side in front of me. I was embarrassed and didn't know what else to say.

"Would you like to come in?"

"Weren't you on your way out?"

"Nah, it can wait."

I nodded shyly when he stepped out and pushed his front door open.

"Okay ..."

I walked in slowly, glanced around me and closed my eyes. I could smell Daniel all around me. I felt safe. I felt familiarity and intimacy. I hankered after him once again.

Daniel closed the door behind me and followed me into the kitchen.

"Wine or coffee?"

"I could really use a glass of wine."

He turned around and took out two glasses. He walked over to his under counter bar and brought out a bottle of wine before he poured us both a glass and sat on the stool in front of me.

I sat down slowly and sipped at the wine.

"So, what's going on?"

"You're going to think I am a terrible person."

"Let me decide ..."

"I told you about Michael, right?"

"Yeah, your ex. The guy we ran into at The Red Velvet?"

I pointed my index finger and winked,

"That one, yes."

I took another sip before I placed my glass on the counter,

"What I didn't tell you was that ever since our divorce became final, he has been texting, calling and showing up at my apartment and the museum non-stop. He has a problem with my vocabulary, the way I dress, and I am pretty sure with anything and everything I do."

"What a prick."

"So, about two months ago, he showed up at my place at five in the morning. I was fuming. But nevertheless, I let him in. Ally Bradshaw had a plan. A supposed flawless plan, or so I thought. I blindfolded him, tied him up and pulled his pants off to expose him, before I walked out of my apartment and left. When I got into the elevator, I called Lily, his new girlfriend, to pick him up."

Daniel burst out laughing and instantly raised his hand,

"Good for you, Ally Bradshaw! High five!"

I lifted my hand and smacked his. I was not as excited as he was, though.

"Well, that's what I thought until my parents called."

"You're kidding. He told your parents?"

"He didn't just tell them, he told my dad that I drugged him."

"Noooooo …"

"I drugged him! So anyway, they've insisted I come home for three weeks and get the help I supposedly need."

"Don't go, Ally."

"I do have to go. If I don't, they'll come here and stay at my place indefinitely. My dad will probably try to perform an exorcism or something like that on me."

"Oh no. Do you want me to come with you?"

"Are you kidding? That will just send my dad over the edge. Besides, you're working."

"I have enough leave saved up."

He was being dead serious. My heart skipped another beat when those butterflies began flapping their wings somewhere deep inside of me. Daniel was nothing like anyone I had ever met before and I couldn't quite put my finger on exactly what it was that set him apart from the rest. There were a million little things.

"Why would you do that, Daniel?"

Daniel took my hand and gently squeezed it,

"Because I care about you, Ally. Because I get why you do what you do. Because, from the very first moment I laid my eyes on you, my heart wouldn't let me forget you."

Alice VL

"Wow. Thank you, Daniel, but I'll be okay."

"Alright, but you call if you need me. I'll come and get you anytime; day or night."

Reliable. Dependable. Caring. They were only but a few words to describe this fireman in that very moment.

I smiled and took another sip of my wine.

"And the good doctor. Didn't you just show up at his place like twenty minutes ago?"

"I did, but then I realized that I wanted to see you. He's leaving to go back to Sutherland tomorrow, and I just wanted to see you. Imagine that?"

"You backed out on a date with a plastic surgeon to drink wine with a fireman?"

"Yup. It looks that way."

"Well, Ally Bradshaw. I wouldn't want to disappoint you."

Daniel got up from his stool and walked over to me. He lifted my chin just enough to meet my eyes. 'There it is.' The look I still couldn't quite put a label on. He took the wine glass from my hand and placed it on the counter.

"You coming?"

"Daniel … I don't know if this is a good idea?"

"It probably isn't."

I DO (NOT) – ON ICE

He lifted me off the stool and placed his arms around me.

"I don't know what this is, Ally, but I do know that you don't want to be tied down. At least, not just yet. I didn't understand it in the beginning, and I am not totally convinced I fully understand it now, but I sort of get it. So, this is what I propose. We remain friends. I want to be your friend. I like what we have too. I like you. Let's just be friends and you know ... enjoy the benefits of our friendship every once in a while."

"No expectations?"

"None whatsoever. If you are seeing someone, I'll back off and if I am, you back off."

I looked into his eyes and frowned. I didn't at all like the idea of him seeing other women.

'How hypocritical of you Ally Bradshaw.'

I was beleaguered by my mixed emotions. It was weighing down heavily on me. I felt defeated, but I didn't want to tell Daniel how I was feeling. I didn't want to create an unrealistic expectation when I myself, couldn't quite decipher my emotions.

"You just don't seem like the kind of guy, Danny?"

"Well, you didn't seem like the kind of woman. Maybe, we just don't really know each other? Maybe being friends is what we need?"

This man was saying all the right things. 'Except for the other women part.' I still needed to process all of that. But not then. Not that night. Not there.

I leaned forward and seized his face into my hands. I kissed him gently and when his tongue crossed over into my mouth, I pressed myself firmly against him. I slipped my arms around his neck and squeeze him protectively against me. I was intensely swept up and enraptured by his scent.

Daniel flinched slightly and grabbed my hand before I followed him down the hall and into his bedroom. When I reached the center of his bedroom, I turned around to face him. He gently brushed my cheek before he untied my hair.

I turned my back to him when he slowly began unzipping my ruby red dress. When it fell to the floor, I gradually turned to back to him. He stepped back and stared at me. His eyes began to inspect every inch of me and I was suddenly slightly embarrassed and totally unnerved.

He moved closer and removed my bra, leaving me totally exposed. When he slid his arms around me, I became self-conscious at once. His eyes gazed into mine before he pulled me closer and kissed me again.

Slowly, he pointed me towards the bed and gently laid me down. With my arms at my side, I stared at him. He was too quiet. Disturbingly quiet.

Daniel removed his shirt and unzipped his jeans. When he was finally as exposed as I was, he slid in next to me and laid down beside me. With his head resting on his elbow, his fingers trickled down from my mouth, to my arms, down my belly before he moved up and down my thighs. I shuddered often and felt goosebumps on every inch of my skin. It felt intimate. Personal. Like love.

His eyes followed his hands while a discreet smile formed around his mouth. He was unobtrusive and took his time. I couldn't help but stare at him, and wonder what he was thinking?

When his eyes found mine, he leaned in closer, placed his hand on my cheek and kissed me again. I wanted him. I wanted to feel his skin on mine and I wanted to feel his body pressed down on mine. I wanted to feel his heartbeat and I wanted to feel his arms around me. I wanted to feel safe again.

I turned him onto his back and climbed on top of him before he again, wrapped his arms around me. Daniel held me tightly and moved slowly. Everything about Daniel was slow, gentle and oh so heavenly at that very moment. His grip tightened around me and I couldn't help but feel how different intimacy was with Daniel. Every inch of my body trembled as I lowered my body onto his and rested my head in his neck.

He felt like home. I laid quietly while he continued to move slowly. He reached down to the small of my back with one hand, holding onto me with his other and pulled me tightly against him. His scent haunted me. My legs tightened suddenly, and my knees squeezed against him. I could feel his body become rigid as he moved slightly faster, gripping at me with all his might.

I whimpered softly into his shoulder when tremors and shudders began to overpower me, leaving me to bite my lower lip so hard, I could taste a droplet of my own blood. Again, a million tiny electrical currents were penetrating every pore of my body.

Alice VL

I DO (NOT) – ON ICE

Daniel quivered below me before he became deathly still and moaned softly before he buried his head in my neck.

"Ally."

His breathing was irregular. My breathing was synchronized with each current rushing through my body. He brought his arms back up and placed it around me before he once again, tightened his grip on me. I could feel his warm breath in my neck as he groaned softly.

For a moment, Daniel and I laid quietly as if frozen in time, waiting for our bodies and breathing to return to normal. When my body finally returned to its natural state, I lifted slightly before he pulled me back down and held me firmly in his arms.

"Not now … wait."

Again, I rested my head in his neck and breathed him in for just a moment longer. I felt tipsy. Drunk. On a high. I was not thinking clearly and indulged in the feel of his skin and his strong, muscular arms around me. I slid my hands in under his shoulders and held onto him. Our hot, sweaty bodies were in sync and I liked the way he felt underneath me. I felt safe. Loved. Wanted. Beautiful. Exciting. Did I say loved?

'No Scratch that.'

I wanted to lay there forever. I wanted to close my eyes and fall asleep in his arms. 'Hang on. What?' I was losing control. Daniel was coming too close to conquering me and my heart was trying to change me. 'No. Not today.'

I lifted my head slightly and moved closer to his ear.

Alice VL

I DO (NOT) – ON ICE

"I've got to go …" He turned his head and touched my lips with his. He kissed me softly and gently stroked my loose flowing, unruly and wild hair.

"I know …"

I smiled sadly. How I wished things were different; how I wished I was different. How I wished I could choose Daniel and spend every remaining day of my life on top of him, or under him.

I had no doubt that Daniel was perfect for me. Faultless. Flawless. But Ally Bradshaw was not quite ready to settle down yet. Ally Bradshaw as not quite equipped to spend the remainder of her days with just one man.

I stared at him, fascinated by him and wholly swept up into his world once again. Mesmerized. Stupefied and absolutely besotted with my fireman.

"I want to lay here for just a moment longer …"

I whispered croakily as I traced his brow, his nose and every single furrow on his face. I didn't want to forget what he looked like at that very moment. Still lying in his folded arms, he squeezed me tighter and held me firmly, as though he was protecting me from the big, bad world out there. I closed my eyes and felt him into my soul. I laid there absorbing every inch of Daniel, afraid that not too long from that very moment, I might forget how I felt at that very second.

Alice VL

I DO (NOT) – ON ICE

With my eyes still closed, I could hear an alarm going off in the distance somewhere. I just wanted to keep them closed. I was warm, comfortable and I could still smell Daniel. The sounds of the alarm grew increasingly louder, and I could feel Daniel shift slightly.

'Did I fall asleep?'

I opened my eyes slowly. They were heavy. Tired. Sluggish. I focused on Daniel and noticed that his eyes were closed too. I lifted my head slightly and realized that the sun was shining through his bedroom window. I quickly glanced around me and realized that were covered by a throw and that we must have fallen asleep, like that.

"Daniel …"

I whispered as softly as I could when I heard him moan. I giggled faintly as I watched him struggle to open his eyes. His cheeks were flustered. His lips were bright red and his hair had a life of its own.

"Did we fall asleep?"

"You did. I figured I'd let you sleep for a while and wake you. I must have dozed off too?"

He reached for his alarm clock and pressed the snooze button in irritation.

"I have to go …"

"Right this very moment?"

Alice VL

I DO (NOT) – ON ICE

I can feel him shift slightly below me, at once magnificently aware of the reaction of my body. I shifted slightly and grinned,

"Shortly …"

I leaned forward and kissed him. He rolled me over and slid his arms in underneath my shoulders. I lifted my legs and folded them around his back before he leaned in to kiss me. I opened my mouth slightly, just enough to welcome his tongue into my mouth.

It was warm. Fleshy. Just the way I liked it. He moved gently, back and forth, up and down. Just the way I liked it. I was instantly aware of my pleasure senses coming back to life again. It suddenly dawned on me that I had never been in such a position first thing in the morning and before as much as a cup of coffee. I liked it. It was different again, but so much more intense. It felt so much more like an awakening; a deeply sensual awakening.

My sensitivity levels were elevated and it didn't take much to be swept up into an alternate universe and lay amongst the stars. I was putty in Daniel's hands each time my body took over and responded to Daniel's touch. Everything about Daniel heightened every single sense, elevating me to new levels each time. I would shake and shudder, my breathing becoming louder, and my voice huskier,

"Daniel …"

His breathing was brasher and rapider, his body firmer and as I disappeared in underneath him, I once again buried my head in his chest.

"Hold me …"

'Ally Bradshaw!'

It had slipped out and I didn't care. Daniel slid his arms in fully underneath me and lifted me up against him. He held onto me as though he was clinging for dear life, all the while it was me clinging to him for dear life.

I felt each muscle on his body tense up and intensify against me. Daniel lowered his head and rested it next to mine, without saying a word or letting out a sound. His eyes were closed and I couldn't help kissing him tenderly on his cheek. His warm, flustered, beautiful cheek. Daniel opened his eyes, not quite wide awake yet, but smiling broadly.

"I really must go."

"I know."

He rolled over at once and ran his fingers through his hair. I laid quietly for just a moment longer before I picked my dress up from the floor and disappeared into his bathroom where I firmly shut the door behind me.

I sponged myself down and quickly slipped into my clothes. I swiftly brushed my hair with a hairbrush that was laying on the vanity. I looked terrible. The little make-up that was left on face was smudged. I rinsed my face and was horrified by the image staring back at me. Not a drop of make-up. Flustered cheeks. Messy hair and a pale skin.

I DO (NOT) – ON ICE

'Why can't I look as good as Daniel does first thing in the morning?'

"Yeah. Right Ally."

I walked out slowly, quietly and nervously. I was not sure if Daniel had actually really looked at me yet. I was panicky.

Like a thief in the night, I peeked into his bedroom and peered over at his unmade bed. He was nowhere to be seen. I rushed over to where my shoes were scattered and quickly slipped them on.

I hurriedly made my way down the ice-cold passage, and when I turned the corner, I noticed Daniel pouring coffee.

"So …"

"Here …"

I apprehensively walked into the kitchen and sat on a bar stool where he handed me a cup of coffee.

"Are you getting cold?"

"So cold. I should've brought something warm."

Daniel smiled before he placed his coffee mug on the counter before me. When he disappeared around the corner, I frowned. Almost at the speed of lightning, he was back and handed me a jacket.

"Here …"

I quickly slid my arms into it. It smelled great. Like Daniel.

Alice VL

I DO (NOT) – ON ICE

Forest. Wood. Rain.

"Thanks. This is so warm."

We sat in silence and when I took my last sip, I got up to leave. I didn't want to leave, but I didn't want to stay either. When I reached his front door, I promptly began taking the jacket off before he stopped me,

"Keep it on. It's cold outside. You can bring it back when you get back from Constantia."

"You sure?"

"Positive. It's insurance."

"Insurance for what?"

"To bring you back here …"

My heart broke out into a flutter once again, leaving me to grin from ear to ear,

"You better believe it."

I placed my arms around his neck and kissed him enthusiastically,

"See you in a few weeks …"

"I can just try and warn the ranchers in Constantia … I have a feeling they're in trouble …"

"I have a feeling you are my greatest trouble …"

I grabbed my bag and turned around. Daniel followed me

opened the front door, and smiled.

"Have a safe trip. Call me if you need me …"

"Thanks Daniel. Just checking … are we okay?"

"Oh, you mean the no strings in the we?"

He burst out laughing and squeezed my hand,

"I actually kinda like this …"

I let out a huge sigh of relief, trying my best not to make it seem too obvious. I couldn't wait to get back and do that all over again.

"Bye."

I waved reservedly before I walked out his door.

"Bye."

I turned back one last time just as Daniel closed his front door. I liked him. A lot. Love? No. Still, I had a sense of loyalty to him; a special place for him. He was a part of me and who I have become. 'No. I don't love him, but I wanted him. Like this.'

"Hmm … I wonder about those eight-second men, ranchers and rodeo guys back home? Constantia … I am coming for one!"

Alice VL

ALMOST THE END!

Can you make head or tails of my unexpected, untaught, un-everything about Daniel, because I can't?

But, I don't want to dwell on him too much, just yet. I am still test-driving my new life and trying to establish my place in this whole new world that Daniel has opened up for me.

I am learning as I go and half the time, I don't think I get it. I don't understand much of any of this, but I am feeling my way through and I am learning more and more about everything, every single day.

My instincts are stronger, my longing for my next rush is just the next encounter away. I am still learning so much about my body, and I am trying figure myself out in the process.

I had so much fun with Doctor Walker. He was different. But for now, he is on ice. He is a little more intense sexually, but Daniel wins each time pleasure-wise. He is warm, caring and gentle where Doctor Walker is a little colder and detached. I don't mind. I liked that about him.

Where all this with Daniel will go, I have no idea? What I do know is that I am not ready to limit myself to just one man. I like my freedom. I like the anticipation of meeting someone new. I like discovering new things about myself with each new man.

Alice VL

I DO (NOT) – ON ICE

But, I don't want to let Daniel go either. I want his fix. I need his high. I need to be me, and Daniel lets me.

I don't know how Michael and I will move forward after this. I admit, I did go a little too far when I called Lily, but at the same time, so did he when he accused me of drugging him and calling my parents merely to punish me.

So now, I am destined to spend the next three weeks with my parents in Constantia and all I can think of are the eight-second men, rodeo guys and ranchers.

Come with me as I spend the next three weeks sneaking out of my parents' farmhouse to rendezvous with an eye-catching rancher called Ryan Henderson who I meet at the Annual Fall Festival.

Discover my father's reaction when we are caught on video and on display for the entire town, the day before I come home to Willow County.

Call me whatever you like, just don't call me drab, boring or ugly!

Ally!

Alice VL

www.ingramcontent.com/pod-product-compliance
Lightning Source LLC
Chambersburg PA
CBHW022022170626
46808CB00003B/1024